RUN FOR YOUR LIFE

BONNIE GREENWOOD GRANT

Disclaimer

The characters in this story are a result of the writer's imagination; with the exception of God, who plays Himself.

Dedication

This book is dedicated to my father, Wendell Carl (Bud) Greenwood, who always encouraged me to be the best I could be;

Acknowledgements

When I walked into the East Cobb Carving Club, the first person I met was Bob Brogan. He not only encouraged me but also introduced me to ELM (Enrichment of Life Movement) and Lloyd Blackwell who brought me to the Christian Authors Guild and my beloved critique group. They were the nest to shelter my fledgling efforts. Without them, my stories would be stuck away in a computer file or, worse, lost in the far reaches of my brain. Judy Becker and Marcus Beavers are the originals members. Cindy Cooper and Roger Elam have replaced Cindy Simmons, Robert Graves, Eddie Snipes, and Jennifer Hanawalt with her famous line, "This is boring, change it."

My thanks to all of you

.

Thanks also to Barbara Key (from ELM) and Myra Beavers for their editing abilities, Ronnie Landau (from ELM) for photo advice, Helen Corbett for police procedures advice and last but certainly not least, Herb and Darnea Moon (from Mt Paren). Herb is my video trailer expert and Darnea is working on my audio book.

They say it takes a village to raise a child, and I might add, it takes combined communities to nurture a writer.

Chapter 1

"Drew! Drew! Drusilllllaaaaa!"

"Oh, great, now what?" Drusilla said to herself. She was upstairs in their bedroom putting away laundry.

"Drusilla!"

She glanced in the mirror as she passed. She saw an attractive, tall, twenty two year old. *Here I am, a senior in college and I don't have the vaguest idea of what I want to do with my life. I have offers from every major graduate school; in four major fields of interest, two journalism jobs offers, and a position on the United States' women's Olympic soccer team, if I want it. I can do anything I want. I can be anything I want, but the catch is, I don't know what I want. Help. I'd like to just stay right where I am, going to school; Bob and I enjoy living with Gran and Papa, with no responsibilities. I guess I just want to stay a kid. Hmmm. I wonder . . .*

"Drew!" Bob bellowed again.

She was about to yell downstairs to ask what he wanted, but decided to go find out.

She smiled and thought about her husband. He was intelligent, kind, loving, and handsome, but since they had been living with her grandparents, Bob had picked up some of Papa's bad habits, such as bellowing for his wife like a bull moose during mating season.

She sighed, picked up the dirty sheets, flipped her reddish brown ponytail over her shoulder and started downstairs to see what the big deal was. "I'm going to have to nip this behavior in the bud," she said loudly.

Bob was running his fingers through his short dishwater blond hair when she came through the doorway. He did this so frequently that it looked spikey. There was always a tuft of hair sticking out somewhere. People said he looked like an adult Dennis the Menace.

"Stop bellowing. What's so doggone important that you couldn't come and talk to me like a normal person?"

He pointed to the TV set, "Your grandmother is on TV."

"My grandmother is always on TV," Drew said.

"Three times is 'always'?"

"Well it seems like always. *And* I don't mind her being on television, as long as she doesn't embarrass me, by standing on her head or some other goofy thing." She stared at the screen, "Oh, no! She *is* standing on her head!"

Bob grabbed the remote and pressed the volume control. Drew started to protest, then thought better of it. She knew Bob still enjoyed the novelty of seeing his grandmother-in-law on television.

Drew's grandmother neatly rolled down from her headstand, stood and walked back to her chair. Gran appeared limber as she moved with the grace of an athlete.

"Look how cute she looks," Bob said.

Her short curly brown hair framed her smiling round face. Gran's hair normally stuck out at all angles like Bob's. Appearance wasn't a priority in either of their lives. Maybe that was one of the reasons they got along so well.

The TV hostess exclaimed loudly. "Mrs. MacIntyre, that was wonderful! You are such an inspiration. And, you still play soccer? Amazing! Stan, would you run that clip?" Drew's grandmother appeared on the screen in her soccer uniform, racing to intercept a high pass. She jumped and used her head to redirect the ball to one of her teammates.

"Oh, Gran, that was incredible. It is all right to call you Gran, isn't it?" asked the TV hostess.

"Of course."

"I would never guess that you were seventy five, not in a million years. I've read your column and you certainly practice what you preach. I understand your clinic's becoming a Mecca for alternative healing."

"Yes it is. It's mushrooming. People are tired of being sick and are tired of medications that have annoying, or even deadly side effects. I know several people who had knee replacements and later found out the sore joints were a side effect of statin drugs (cholesterol lowering drugs).

"We believe inflammation disorders such as diabetes, heart disease and Alzheimer's are caused by synthetic and processed foods. Have you ever read a label on Pop Tarts? I defy you to find anything of nutritional value in it. It's a non-food.

"Kids don't drink milk any more. Cola is the drink of choice. The 'complete meal' consists of a white flour bun with all sorts of dough conditioners and preservatives, a piece of meat with herbicides (weed killers), pesticides (bug killers), and hormones (to make a fatter steer and which makes your children go through puberty long before they're ready to), french fries (which make your blood sugar spike faster and higher than pure sugar), and a cola. I have a friend who is a stewardess. People with babies often hand her a baby bottle and ask her to fill it with cola. You see we have our work cut out for us." Gran said.

"I can understand avoiding non-foods to prevent problems, but what about those of us who already have high cholesterol? How do we lower it?"

"That's a loaded question, because cholesterol is needed for your body to function and the drug companies have fostered the misinformation that all cholesterol is bad. What is bad is the inflammation that causes your arteries to weaken and tear. Your body uses the cholesterol as a bandage. Your liver makes cholesterol and your brain is made of it. In fact, one study showed that if your cholesterol levels got below 250 you could start having memory loss. It doesn't make a lot of sense to prescribe a drug that interferes with the liver's function so that the cholesterol number will go down when cholesterol is not the problem, the inflammation is.

"In answer to your question, if your cholesterol is high, eat grapefruit, but not while you're taking a statin drug. You need to increase your fiber intake; a teaspoon of whole flax seed, apples with peels, oranges with pulp; you get the idea. I dropped my cholesterol 100 points in three months with a teaspoon of whole golden flax seed sprinkled on a half of red organic grapefruit.

"The number you want to worry about is 'one'." Gran said.

"Now you've really lost me," the woman said.

"One or less should be the score on your CRP test. CRP stands for C - reactive protein. It measures the inflammation in your body and is the most accurate test to warn of an impending heart attack or diabetes. Inflammation is your first line of defense. However, sometimes your body doesn't know when to back off and the inflammation stays and gets in the way. When we eat wrong or don't exercise it causes our body to malfunction. Cod liver oil, that old standby from my generation, works well to lower inflammation.

"Most doctors are too busy to do much research after they start their practices so they often only hear about *health* information from the drug reps. Have you ever been to the doctor's office and seen the drug reps perched near the receptionist's desk like vultures, waiting to see the doctors?

"Make no mistake. Drug companies do not want you to be healthy. There is no profit for them if you are well, because healthy people don't need drugs.

"In my *non-profit* clinic we have a program where people come in for two weeks and we teach them to eat right. We teach them to eat real food, organic, whole grain bread, free range chicken, grass-fed beef, wild caught salmon, low mercury tuna fish, and fruits and vegetables, *lots* of fruits and vegetables. We evaluate their body types and problems. We boost their immune systems and put them on a regimen of exercise and food that is designed just for them. Often their health is restored to the point where they are eventually able to get off all prescription drugs."

"It's hard to imagine that people can get well just by changing the food they eat," the hostess said.

Drew grabbed the controller from Bob's hand and turned the television off.

Bob gave her a hurt look. "Why did you do that?"

"I've heard it my whole life. 'Oh, honey, your body has to last you a lifetime. You need to take care of it.'"

Bob took the sheets from her arms, laid them on the back of the couch and encircled her with his arms.

"And you did such a good job. I really like your body."

"Bob," she protested as he leaned down to kiss her.

"We're married." He felt her smile against his lips as he kissed her. He looked up. "What are you grinning about?

"I did let you talk me into marrying you, didn't I?" she said, as she smiled and looked into his incredibly blue eyes.

"It was the best decision you ever made," he said as he grinned back.

Chapter 2

Drew finally found a parking space in the crowded university parking lot. As usual the parking spot was on the outskirts of civilization. Two options for making it to class on time presented themselves. She could run to class and arrive hot and sweaty, or she could use her bicycle and arrive calm and cool; so the bike was the perfect solution. At first it she felt strange riding her bike, but when she saw how many others were doing it, she stopped feeling quite so self-conscious. It was downhill to the psychology building so it took her only seconds to get there, lock her bike and run up the steps to her physiology class.

I love this class. Having Gran for a grandmother doesn't hurt because she always shares the latest articles and studies on health so I often know more than the teacher. She was careful not to reveal her grandmother's identity. She didn't want to be teased by her classmates about being related to the *health lady–especially* since her own choice of snacks ranged from Captain Crunch to an occasional candy bar.

As usual, class flew. It was over before she realized it, and she was in the stream of students on their way to their next class. *It's wonderful. It's like a river of knowledge and I'm part of it. I feel like a salmon swimming upstream, only instead of swimming upstream to spawn, I'm seeking knowledge.* There was so much she wanted to learn.

As she pulled into the driveway, Gran pulled in right beside her. Gran's choice of transportation was also a source of embarrassment. She either drove Papa's teal-colored truck or she drove her grandson Jeremy's 4x4 Jeep Grand Cherokee.

Drew vividly remembered her cousin's lecture, "You're being silly. You shouldn't be embarrassed by Gran's choice of transportation. It has nothing to do with you."

But he's not living here. And he bought a newer more conventional car for work after graduation so he obviously thought the Jeep was not dignified or maybe he's just saying he doesn't see anything wrong with a 75 year old grandmother driving a Jeep equipped with an off-road kit; complete with big tires, brush guards, step up bars and fog lights. The bars are supposed to protect the vehicle, but Drew laughed when she remembered the time Papa backed the Jeep into a neighbor's mailbox and broke the rear light. The bars didn't help protect anything. In fact, Drew thought it was the bar bending into the light that broke it.

"Hey, Gran" she called. Then she noticed how tired her grandmother looked. Her dad always called Gran Odie (the bouncy dog in the Garfield comic strip), because she was so full of energy. This afternoon though, her bright blue eyes didn't sparkle and her short brown hair drooped; even the freckles sprinkled across the bridge of her nose looked faded.

"You look terrible."

"You have such a way with words," Gran quipped. "Be nice or I'll pull out my soapbox and start lecturing on nutrition or God or better yet, *both.*"

"No, please, I'm sorry." Drew pleaded in mock horror. "Seriously, Gran, what's wrong?"

"Did you see any of that talk show yesterday?" Gran asked.

"A little."

"Well, I need to take communication classes before I go on the air. Our web site was flooded. The phones rang constantly."

"Isn't that good?"

"Well, it would have been if the calls were for reservations and information. But they weren't. Government agencies called, wanting to come out and check our facilities. It seems someone from the drug companies saw the show and called their lobbyist, who in turn, stormed the House and Senate about my misleading the public. Then a horrid man called me and threatened to have me thrown in jail. He started yelling, 'Woman, don't you realize that most people need to stay on these drugs for the rest of their lives?' I responded that while the drug company's financial bottom line would probably be healthier if people took the drugs for the rest of their lives, but the people who were strong-armed into taking drugs they didn't need would not be healthier. I have proved that over and over. Drugs are not the answer. Those silly drug companies pitched a fit to the government agencies and complained about my supposed policy of taking all patients off their medication. I told them that we never touch their medication. We just work on getting them healthy. I mean, people die every day from drugs. One of the drugs they prescribe is Warfarin, a deadly rat poison, under the name Coumadin, to thin the blood, and they have the audacity to yell at me for endangering people's lives? I have a friend from high school who started bleeding internally from the drug and almost died. The drug companies neglected to tell the doctors and nurses to encourage eating greens and adjust the dose accordingly. Judy was told to avoid greens. Boy, do they have, what's the Spanish word for balls?"

Drew almost choked. "Gran, you *must* be upset." Drew couldn't stop the grin that spread across her face.

Her grandmother blushed, "Oops, sorry, that was rather crude. I apologize."

"You know what Papa always says, 'Sorry isn't good enough.'" Drew said smugly.

Gran narrowed her eyes, "Do I need to take you on, too?"

"You'd threaten your grandchild? Shame on you, and after all this talk about respecting me and my ideas. Wait till I tell Mom and Dad."

"You'd rat me out? Maybe I'm lucky your dad was transferred to another state, although I really miss them." She looked at Drew and wagged her head. "Why am I fighting this losing battle? I'm just too tired. Here I am being harassed as I walk into my own house that I *graciously* share rent- free with you and Bob. He is always a joy. But sometimes Drew, you are exasperating. One minute you are the most annoying child possible, to the point of rudeness. Then when you see what hurt your words have caused, you are immediately contrite. You are like your dad in that respect. He will say something thoughtless, then, he realizes that he's hurt you and be sorry.

Drew ran to her grandmother, cradled her cheek and said, "I've done it again, haven't I? I'm sorry; I didn't mean to offend you."

"Oh, Drew, I'm just tired, and a little depressed. I also got calls from people that thought we could cure cancer in two weeks. They were so desperate, especially if they were calling for a loved one. I tried to explain that we couldn't do miracles. I told them that only God can cure cancer immediately. All we can do is teach them how to restore health so that their bodies can function the way they were designed. There were no guarantees. We lose some, not many, I'll grant you, but we can't save all of them. If God decides it's time for you to go, you go. All the antioxidants, Transfer Factor and other immune boosters in the world aren't going to stop His plan for you. People have to realize that." She sighed as she continued up the front porch steps. "I hate it when I mess up. I could be in big trouble."

Drew came over and put her arm around her grandmother's shoulders. Drew was 5'9" and her grandma was 5'5" so she had to lean down. She made a big show of it.

"You smart alecky child. I would have been taller if my mother hadn't threatened to put a brick on my head, to keep me from growing taller than 5'5"—her idea of the perfect height for a woman. She was 5'6" and that was very tall for a woman of her era.

Gran put her arm around Drew's slim waist. "You know I only want the best for you, don't you, Honey?"

"Yes Gran, I know you do. I am lucky to have someone like you. I know you pray for us every day and you always try to help us develop into the brightest, healthiest, holiest, and most creative people we can be." With that comment, Drew kissed her Gran's forehead and they went into the house.

"I'll have to remember that for next time, when I want to avoid a health or God lecture." Drew said cheekily.

Drew ducked and laughed as Gran threw a sofa pillow at her.

"What's for dinner?" Drew asked before she thought about it. She knew Gran was designated cook, but momentarily forgot how tired her grandmother was.

"I called Papa before I left. It won't be the healthiest meal in the world but it'll be wonderful because *I* won't have to fix it."

Just then the phone rang.

"I'll get it. Mmmm, something smells good."

It was Bob. "Hi, Honey," she said and smiled. He was having car problems.

"Papa," Drew yelled. "Bob needs you to come and help him. He thinks it's the water pump." Bob knew a lot about cars, but Papa knew even more. Papa could fix anything. Of course he had to yip about it first, mutter, "Can't anyone fix things besides me?" Then he'd grab his tools, and rush to the rescue like Super Mechanic.

Gran smiled at Drew, "He loves being needed. Don't let him try to fool you."

"Go ahead and eat. I'm not sure how long it's going to take," Papa said as he headed for his truck with his tools in hand. He obviously expected this to be a big job. As he drove out of the driveway, Drew closed the door behind him and turned toward her grandmother, "Gran, I think I will go ahead and eat, because I need to go back to school. I had to request some serious research books through the school library for my term paper that I can 't check out."

Chapter 3

It was getting dark when Drew started to back out of the driveway. Suddenly Gran ran out the front door, calling, "Drew, wait!" Drew rolled the window down. "What's the matter?"

"Your left front headlight is out. If you want, you can take my Jeep."

Drew rolled her eyes. "Boy, this is my lucky day. I just love driving the 'Hulk'." She switched cars and left for the library.

After retrieving her research books from the librarian, she settled at one of the square library tables and began the arduous process of reading through pages and pages of technical jargon. Surprisingly, the research on testosterone and the developing embryo, proved to be fascinating, so time went by quickly. She realized it was getting late when she looked around and saw that she was the last one, besides the librarian, still in the library. Gathering her papers, she felt very pleased at what she had accomplished.

She went down the stairs, pushed open the library doors and started toward her car. The big doors locked behind her. The air was damp and cool and leaves crunched beneath her feet releasing their autumn scent. What *a great night for a run.*

Thirty feet away traffic whooshed by on the other side of the chain link fence. Her car was parked near the fence. She heard muffled voices across the parking lot. Were the sounds coming from near her car? She stopped walking so she could hear. She peered into the shadows and saw movement. Somebody was crouched next to her car. Something shiny reflected the light from the street lamp; a silver buckle, a mirror? Her eyes adjusted. She realized there were two men kneeling beside her front tire. She pulled out her cell phone and started to dial 911 as she yelled at them. "Hey, get away from my car! I'm dialing the police!"

"Should we get her?" She heard one dark figure ask the other.

"I just took pictures of you. I sent them to the police department," she bluffed. She had no idea how to e-mail pictures from her phone.

The two men looked at her, then each other. "Let's get out of here," one muttered. After a moment's hesitation, they stood and ran toward a truck parked haphazardly behind the Jeep. The truck sputtered once, then started, leaving stinking exhaust in its wake as it roared toward the exit.

Were they gone? They were gone, weren't they? Oh, God, please let them be gone. She crept closer to the car and clicked the key remote. When the lights came on inside the car, she ran the rest of the way, jerked the door open, threw her books and body inside then pulled the door shut and locked it. She started the engine and set a record for backing up.

As the Jeep roared out to the street, her eyes searched the parking lot, then the oncoming traffic, for the sight of a truck coming back for her. *Please, God, let them be gone.* She continued to glance in her rear view mirror. She still expected the truck, at any moment, to come roaring out of a side street or dirt driveway, after her. *Get a grip* she told herself, but her eyes searched each truck that came near.

It was then that she noticed the flapping white paper stuck under her windshield wiper. She pulled over, rolled down the driver's side window, reached out and pulled the paper inside. After making the turn into her subdivision, she slowed, opened the folded note, reached up and turned on the overhead light. She gasped, took her eyes off the road, and then looked up just in time to swerve away from a mailbox. The note was hand printed in big block letters on the back of a lost dog flyer: NEX TIME WE WONT JUST CUT YOR TIRES. NEX TIME WE CUT YOU!!!!

Her foot slammed the brake against the floor. She recalled the flash of light that she'd seen in the parking lot. That might have been the reflection from a knife blade. They had knives! *But they couldn't have cut my tires because they're not flat. Brilliant deduction, Drew.* As the reality of what happened started to sink in, she began to tremble. She could be lying somewhere in a pool of blood. "Oh, Mama, Daddy, Jesus, help me."

The brake was released and the car continued around the corner, up her street and into the driveway. She was relieved to see Bob, Papa and Gran standing in front of Bob's car with the hood up. They were leaning over the front bumper and looking into the engine. Gran was holding a flashlight over the engine compartment. They looked surprised when Drew slammed the car into park, threw open the door and flew into Bob's arms. She was sobbing so much her body shook. Bob wrapped his arms around her and held her against his chest. "Oh, baby, what has happened to you? It's OK." He rocked her back and forth as she cried. "You're trembling. I've never seen you afraid of anything before."

Papa and Gran moved closer as if trying to protect her. Drew looked up and met Gran's eyes. Drew shoved the crumpled note into Gran's hand. Gran smoothed the note out and held it in front of her flashlight to read it. A frown of concern crossed her face. She turned back to Drew and asked, "Where did this come from?"

Bob reached out for the note. He took the paper, with one arm still protectively wrapped around Drew, and leaned into the light to read it. He laid it on the fender and ran his hand though his hair. "What happened?"

Drew tried to stay coherent as she related the incident.

He hugged her tighter and said, "What I can't figure out is, why you?" He could still feel her shaking. "It's OK. Don't be afraid. I won't let anyone hurt you."

Going inside, they headed directly to the den, with the exception of Papa, who swung past the kitchen refrigerator and grabbed a beer to help him think better. Gran lit the gas fireplace, curled up in an armchair and waited for the others to settle.

Papa started asking questions. Drew hated it when Papa went into interrogation mode because he made her really think about everything that happened. Once he got his teeth into something, he was tenacious as a bulldog. He would not let go. Just when she thought he was coming to the end, he would start on another line of questioning. "How tall do you think they were? What kind of accent did they have? How old do you think they were? Did they move like old or young men? Did they mention you by name?"

How does he think of all these questions? I heard he was an excellent IRS agent and now I know why. Finally he finished. Drew felt totally drained.

Everyone was quiet for a while, occasionally, someone else would ask a question, trying to make sense of what had happened.

"They must have made a mistake. There's no reason to threaten you." Gran said. She looked over at Drew and saw, in her mind's eye, a small terrified child. *Lord, it's not fair. She's come so far. She's overcome all her childhood fears and now this has to happen. Help her get through this with minimal damage.*

A scene from the past flashed into her mind: a four-year-old Drew clutching her hand as they stood on the sidelines of a Disney World ride, watching the rest of the family zoom past, laughing and screaming excitedly. Drew had been terrified of the fast rides, "Thank you for staying with me, Grandma. I'm trying not to be afraid," she had whispered.

Gran was also there six months later, when Drew overcame her terror. She was five and she decided that she was going to ride a neighborhood roller coaster. She got on and gripped the rail with both hands. When the roller coaster came to the top, she deliberately raised her hands like the other kids and although her face went white, she still had a smile pasted on it when she reached the bottom. Her mom and Gran not only clapped and cheered, but Gran took Drew's picture standing on the roller coaster steps with her hands raised in victory. Gran's eyes filled with tears. *She'll conquer this too.*

Brushing the tears away with her fingertips, Gran went over to Drew, sat down beside her and hugged her. "All these questions and comments are not helping your state of mind. I, for one, am going to the kitchen to make some Chamomile tea to help me relax and get some sleep. Would you like some too?"

Bob helped Drew get up. "Come on Sweetheart, let's go up to bed. We'll sort it all out tomorrow. First thing in the morning we'll go in and talk to my brother, Greg, at the Police Department and see what the professionals can come up with."

"I want to drink my tea first," Drew protested. "Gran's right; I need a cup of tea to help me relax. Otherwise, I won't have a prayer of getting to sleep. I'm still shaking."

Chapter 4

While Drew fell asleep as soon as she snuggled in his arms, Bob didn't sleep well at all. All night he kept thinking about what could have happened. He had faith in his physical prowess, at six two, 190 pounds, he had always been able to take care of himself, but when Drew was on her own, how could he protect her? Last night could have been a disaster. Endless possibilities flooded his mind. They could have beaten, raped or even killed her, stabbing and leaving her to bleed to death; or if they'd succeeded in cutting her tires, she could have lost control of the car.

It was a relief when Drew got up to take her shower. He'd lain in bed long enough. *I need to get moving, and boy, do I need coffee. Thank goodness Gran stopped lecturing me on the acidity of it, hallelujah. Now I can savor it in peace.* He shuffled downstairs toward the kitchen. As he neared the bottom of the stairs, he saw Gran in the living room. She was sitting on the couch drinking a cup of herbal tea (she always drank herbal tea in the morning), her

Bible opened on the couch beside her. The two Siamese cats vied for position on her lap. Although he knew it was her prayer time and that she didn't like to be interrupted, she *was* looking up at him. He couldn't resist, "Any messages from God?" He teased.

"Be not afraid, I am with you always," she said without hesitation. Then she said, "Bob, I think they were after me, not Drew. After all, it was my Jeep. They must have thought I was in the library. Why would they threaten an innocent college student with a note? I know young girls are targets for sick men but to leave a note threatening to kill her. For what? Drew doesn't march or demonstrate against anything. Although, she does mouth off occasionally".

Bob's eyebrows rose quizzically as if asking, "Just occasionally?"

"Of course she *was* the highest scorer in her college soccer game last Saturday, as you well know, but I doubt if American soccer fans are as rabid as the Columbian soccer fans. Do you remember the World Cup when the Columbian player accidentally scored on his own goal and Columbia lost to the U.S.?"

Bob hesitated a moment. "If I remember correctly, they *killed* him. However, I don't think it was rabid soccer fans that attacked your Jeep." Bob scratched his head. "I had thought about the drug companies trying to scare you, but that doesn't make much sense either. They would never do something like that; besides the clinic is small and I doubt you upset them enough for them to send someone out to scare you. And, if they think a little note would keep *you* quiet, they better think again. " He grinned at her. "But," he said, sobering, "I do think you were the target. With your license plate proclaiming 'L Chayim', 'to life' in Hebrew, how could they miss it? He hurried on with his thought, "Most people probably wouldn't know what that meant, but on last week's interview, the hostess kept going on about how appropriate that license plate was for you. 'To life', not only for finding cures for ailing people, but for the unborn and the aged. So the question remains, *who* is after you?" He continued, "I called my brother Greg last night. Drew and I are going down to his office at 10:00 AM."

"What about work?" Gran asked.

"I called and told them I'd be late. They said to take as long as I needed. I wouldn't be able to concentrate on investments if I'm worried about Drew."

"Bob, do you think Drew might have gotten a picture? I get pretty good pictures from my phone," Gran said.

"I'm way ahead of you. I thought about that too, and checked them last night," Bob said. "The pictures were pretty dark but I think the police can do something with them."

Papa came down the stairs in time to hear the comment about the police. "Bob, I'd like to go, too. But first I'm going to the auto parts store. I want to replace Drew's headlight." He looked over at Gran, "Penny, I think they might have been after you. I want you to start being more careful."

Drew appeared at the top of the stairs, her hair was slightly damp from her shower. She came and rested her chin on Papa's shoulder hugging him from behind. "I love you, Papa."

He put his hands over hers and kissed her arm.

"However," she said as she jumped the last three steps to the floor, "I have decided that those losers are going down." She feigned some karate moves, being careful not to hit anyone in the crowded hallway.

Trying not to laugh, Bob said, "That would certainly make me think twice before approaching you."

Papa left to get the headlight for Drew's car and Bob helped him install it. At 9:45 AM, they all piled into the Jeep and drove to the police station. They tried to be careful of the doors in case there were fingerprints. Drew was feeling rather foolish, now that it was daylight and with her own vigilante group surrounding her. It was a good thing she hadn't called her mom and dad. They would have driven all night and brought most of her aunts and uncles. Instead of a Jeep Cherokee they'd have to charter a bus. Drew smiled at the thought.

When they arrived at the police station and got out of the car, Papa led the way up the marble stairway. They trooped down the hall to Greg's office. Drew knew that Papa wanted to make sure that the investigation was done right, even though Greg was doing them a favor. She didn't think that a crime had actually been committed. There was only a note and maybe some fingerprints. *Could you arrest someone for writing a threatening note?*

Greg asked the family to wait outside while he talked privately with Drew. Greg and Drew came out of the office together. "OK, this is the way I see it." Greg said. "I agree with you that the perpetrators saw Gran's Jeep and thought they'd get even with her. They were upset with her about something but we just don't know what it was. They don't seem to be too bright but that doesn't preclude them from being violent. My best idea is to give the pictures to the newspapers to see if anyone recognizes them. The lab tells me that while the pictures are dark, we can lighten them up enough so that some one might recognize them. We've taken the prints from the note; at least what prints were left after someone crumpled and then smeared their own prints all over the paper." He gave the whole group a dirty look. They all looked sheepish. "My instinct says that they aren't much of a threat. What do you think about leaking the idea that Gran was threatened? They don't have to know they got the wrong person. They'll think they accomplished their purpose, which they did. I think they saw your Jeep and decided on the spur of the moment to try to scare you."

"What if you are wrong and they really are after Drew. We need to know who to protect," Papa complained.

"Well, the sooner we get those pictures out; the sooner we may have an identification. We will alert campus police to keep an eye on Drew, and I can have an officer do an occasional drive by through your neighborhood." Greg's phone buzzed. "Yes? OK, thanks." He looked back at the expectant faces, "They're finished with the Jeep."

As they came out into the sunlight, Drew looked at the Jeep." I *guess* they're finished with the Jeep," Drew said. "Just look at it, the poor thing looks like it's been through a dust storm."

Chapter 5

Drew walked into class the next afternoon and headed for her usual seat at one of the front tables. Not wanting to miss anything, she always sat near the front. She immediately sensed a change in the room's atmosphere. All talking ceased and no one met her eyes.

Her greetings were met with silence instead of the usual repartee. Sharon, a petite brunette with spiked hair and large intelligent brown eyes, was the first to break the silence. "Why didn't you tell us that the healing lady was your grandmother? No wonder you knew all this cell biology stuff. Were you scared?"

Drew stopped in the act of pulling her chair out and looked at Sharon. "What are you talking about?"

"It's in the morning paper." Sharon shoved an opened newspaper across the table toward her.

"Oh, my goodness," was all Drew could think to say. There were pictures of Gran's Jeep and two pictures from her cell phone that showed two crouching men and the second picture showed the two men standing. "Boy, are they scruffy looking. Does anyone recognize them?" she asked.

"I think your grandmother is just looking for more publicity for her fake clinic," said Wayne, one of her classmates who usually sat at her table.

Drew turned her head sharply toward him and demanded, "So you're saying that my grandmother hired someone to scare me to death?"

"What do you mean, 'scare you to death?' What do you have to do with it?"

"I was the one driving the Jeep. The police wanted the guys who did it to think that they had succeeded in scaring Gran." Drew said.

"Well, you could have been in on it," Wayne said.

Drew's mouth dropped open. "You know Wayne, I *used* to like you." Drew looked down at her classmate. "I can't believe that you'd accuse my grandmother of fraud, or whatever it is you're accusing her of. There are a lot of people who have been healed in her clinic, true miracle healings, many in stage four cancers, people whose doctors have sent them home to die." She glared at him. She would have liked to leap across the table and strangle the little rat, but he was smaller than she was. She might really damage him if she got her hands too near his throat.

Jon didn't make things any better. "I half agree with Wayne."

Drew spun her head back and glared at *him.*

"I don't believe she set up the 'attack', or that she deliberately deceives people," Jon said, "but let's face it, most of her publicity comes from her physical condition. It's not every seventy-five year-old lady that can run around a soccer field. She has good genes. My grandfather lived to be 90. He smoked like a chimney and drank a quart of beer every night. He had good genes. It's the same with your grandmother, and I don't think it's right to tell people that they'll be able to do the things she does simply by eating differently."

Drew was thunderstruck. "But she *doesn't* have good genes. Gran's got bad papery skin, a malformed back and a congenital heart condition for which she was hospitalized twenty years ago. Every health benefit she has, she has worked hard to achieve."

Jon was skeptical. "If her heart's so bad how come she plays soccer when the exertion could kill her and, anyway, how do you know she has heart trouble?"

Drew searched her memory. "She didn't know she had anything wrong with her heart. A friend of hers who had studied iridology looked into Gran's eyes and told her that she had a congenital heart condition. Gran didn't believe her because nothing ever showed up during any of Gran's checkups.

"Gran started taking bovine thyroid supplements because she always had to watch her weight. She was delighted that with the supplements, she could eat anything she wanted and still lose weight. However, over a week's time her pulse rate went from 52 to 106. She should have known better, but that was twenty years ago. Anyway, one morning as she was taking her cup of tea out of the microwave, she blacked out. Papa found her unconscious on the kitchen floor. He rushed her to the emergency room. The doctors heard a serious heart murmur. Her poor heart couldn't handle the stress of the thyroid stimulation. They kept her in the hospital under observation for several days. As soon as the bovine thyroid worked its way out of her system, the murmur faded.

"It took about two months for her to get a clean bill of health, but now that she knows it's there, she takes supplements to strengthen her heart. She tries to protect it the best she can.

Contrary to popular opinion, 'resting' is not good for a heart. My papa's cardiologist says, 'sitting around on your rear end is like signing your death warrant'. My grandmother uses exercise to help strengthen her heart. Soccer is excellent exercise and besides, she says she wants to die with her soccer cleats on."

When she had finished, no one said a word. Even the teacher stood quietly at her podium.

"Boy, do I know how to bring down the house, or what?" Drew mumbled to herself.

"Drew," her teacher said, "Class, could I have your attention for a minute? Drew brought up an important point." She waited while the class turned their attention to her. "We are not locked into a physical condition just because we may inherit a tendency toward something. There is too much research showing the benefits of proper diet and exercise to doubt that we can improve our health and physical well-being. I just had a thought. Drew, do you think your grandmother would come in and be our guest lecturer?"

Drew rolled her eyes. *Oh, no. What have I done?*

Drew sighed, "I guess. Just leave her a message. She's good about returning calls."

"Class, how many of you would be interested in Drew's grandmother coming to lecture?"

The majority of the class raised their hands. Drew was surprised to see Wayne and Jon's hands among them.

Chapter 6

The Hexal Drug Company was located in downtown Atlanta. Eighteen stories of dark glass pointed into the clear blue sky. On the sixteenth floor, in the conference room, the polished wood and upholstery smelled of leather and lemon. Fifteen people were seated around the mahogany table. Two women, dressed in black power suits, wearing small gold earrings and sporting the same short haircut, were seated together on the far side of the table. The lead chair was empty. As the group waited, they fidgeted with their folders and notes.

The door opened, and Mr. Fitzsimmons, the company CEO, entered the room. He wore a casual blue knit shirt and khaki pants, in marked contrast to the others who looked like morticians in dark suits, white shirts and conservative ties. His brown-black eyes scanned his employees' faces. Many of his employees likened them to the black holes in outer space that sucked in all available matter. He was clean-shaven. On any other man, his face would have been handsome. His friends, if he had any, might have greeted him with smiles of welcome. No one greeted this man with happy smiles. His serious face had frown lines that molded into a scowl around his mouth.

"Let's start," he said. "Barnes, you're our hot-shot sales executive; what do you have?"

"Well, sales are down slightly, which is to be expected because of the cholesterol drug recall. People's memories are short, and as long as we can keep the doctors behind us, our sales should rebound. Regardless, we have Tom, and everyone knows Tom is a genius at coming up with ads that take people's minds off the dangers. Isn't that right, Tom?" Barnes asked.

"It's not that you want them to forget the dangers. Drugs are powerful tools to keep people alive, and because they *are* powerful, if used incorrectly, in the wrong combinations, or the wrong circumstances, they can be deadly. For example, all statin drugs interfere with liver function because the liver makes cholesterol and the brain needs cholesterol to function. So we need to walk a fine line. We emphasize the benefits of the drug, health, happiness, etc—but also remind them to be aware of the side effects. We sell some pretty toxic products," Tom said.

"If you weren't the best at convincing people to buy our products, I might have second thoughts about keeping you on the payroll. I think an attitude realignment might be refreshing. We're not the bad guys," Fitzsimmons said.

He turned back to Barnes, "Then you don't think that 'old bat' has been a factor in our sales drop?"

Barnes looked dumbfounded. "Old bat? Old bat? I'm sorry but . . . oh, do you mean the lady that operates the alternative health clinic?"

"Oh course that's who I mean. Could she be a factor in our loss of sales?" Fitzsimmons demanded again.

"Well, I suppose she could be, but I don't think she'd have any lasting effect, because her methods take time and discipline, and most people want instant results. They might try, say, flax seed for high cholesterol for a while, but flax seed takes 30-60 days to bring down the numbers and most people can't or won't wait that long," Barnes said.

"But don't they have to wait that long even with prescription drugs?" one of the women blurted out. She blanched at the glare Fitzsimmons gave her.

Barnes hesitated.

Tom took a deep breath and said, "Well, that is partially true, but when a man or woman leaves the doctor's office, they usually realize that they're going to be on those drugs forever. They're on a health regimen. "They are on the road to health and all they have to do is pop a pill and remember, it's their doctor who says that it's the way to go."

"Mr. Savage, you are treading on thin ice," Fitzsimmons snarled at Tom.

He turned his wrath on a stately looking gentleman sitting near the head of the table, "Dr Claremont, I want that old bat checked out. Do you think you can manage that?" Fitzsimmons demanded.

Dr. Claremont turned his intelligent hazel eyes on Fitzsimmons. He raised an inquisitive eyebrow at the company's CEO.

"I want this woman's history checked out. Find a serious health condition, one that will ruin her credibility or even kill her," Fitzsimmons said as he strode from the window back to the chair near the head of the table.

"For the record," Dr. Claremont said, "You pay me to set up conferences for doctors to familiarize them with your products, not to research people's medical records."

The look Fitzsimmons gave Dr. Claremont could have begun an immediate ice age.

Dr Claremont hesitated then nodded, "Of course I can pull her medical records."

"Wait a minute; you are not serious, are you?" Tom asked. "Jack LaLanne has been saying the same thing she's been saying, and for a lot longer. He's ninety something and still going strong. I would think he's more of a threat than Gran is." Tom argued.

"Gran? Do you know the woman personally?" Fitzsimmons demanded.

"No, but I'd like to. Everyone calls her Gran. For Pete's sake, she's not in competition with us. She doesn't sell products. She's just a nice little old lady who's trying to get us to eat our vegetables." Tom sounded exasperated.

Barnes added, "I agree that we're making a mountain out of a molehill. If there is a drop in sales because of her, it will be short-lived. As I said previously, not many people can live a perfect lifestyle. We go great for a while and then we fall off the wagon, so to speak. One reason my mom loved Jack LaLane was because he was on TV every day encouraging her. She felt like she had an exercise buddy. She never missed a day when she was pregnant with me. That's why I'm so good-looking and smart," he paused for the expected laughs. Only Tom smiled back at him. He continued, a little shaken, "He makes us happy with the knowledge that it can be done. But his self-discipline is incredible. The average person just won't work that hard. When there is a choice between walking on a cold rainy day or sitting in front of ball game on TV, guess what wins? Even if staying in the chair, I'm quoting my doctor here, 'sitting on your rear is like signing your death warrant.' Consistent exercise takes a lot of effort."

"Gran is easier to identify with. She struggles with her weight, has to trick herself into working out, and can't bring Halloween candy into the house or she'll eat it. Now that's something to which I can relate," Tom said. It was only when he looked around the room that he realized that he had made the situation worse. "Come on, you guys, she's just a little old lady," he protested.

"Yeah, a little old lady who just happens to be on national television and writes a syndicated newspaper column telling people to avoid our products," one of the suits said.

"I am in total agreement, Mr. Myers. Thank you for your support. This meeting is over." Mr. Fitzsimmons turned on his heels and left the room.

Tom looked over at Barnes with a stricken look on his face. Barnes just shrugged. They left the conference room quietly and went into Barnes' office.

"What the hell happened in there?" Barnes asked. "The man's insane. I mean, I like money as much as the other guy, but to want a sweet little old lady knocked off because she may have cost you a couple of bucks is crazy."

"So you think he's serious?" Tom asked.

"It does sound a little far out," he paused, with a thoughtful look on his face. Then he shook his head, "No, he's just ranting. Still it was disturbing. He was very convincing."

"We're being overly suspicious," Tom said.

"Yeah, we're becoming paranoid." Barnes said.

"We're watching too much TV."

"Where do you want to eat lunch?" Barnes asked.

"How about the little Italian place on the corner?" Tom said.

"Sounds good to me," Barnes replied.

Chapter 7

The next time Fitzsimmons met with his team, Barnes and Savage were not included. Dr. Clermont sat in Fitzsimmons's office with a file folder on his lap. His secretary had worked overtime to get all the information in the folder for him. Three other men and one woman sat in the room with him.

"Well, what did you find? Could we be so lucky that she's dying of cancer or that she's a heart attack waiting to happen?" Fitzsimmons demanded.

"That's a little harsh, don't you think?" Dr. Claremont asked.

"No, I detest the woman, and if I can discredit her, I will."

Claremont thought, *discredit her, he just wants to discredit her-- I can live with that.* He opened his file with a relieved sigh. "She has a congenital heart condition. She was hospitalized about 20 years ago. She had a bout with high cholesterol, but that's down now, blood-pressure is great."

"Tell me about her heart condition. What is a congenital heart condition?"

"In her case, it just means that she was born with a weak heart. Put enough stress on her heart and it could possibly stop beating."

"So that's what happened 20 years ago? What caused her heart to malfunction?" Fitzsimmons asked.

"Bovine thyroid. She was using it as a diet aid and it overstressed her heart. I don't imagine a stun gun would be too good for her either." Dr. Clermont winced to himself. *I wish I hadn't said that.*

Chapter 8

Drew threw her backpack over the stair railing and exploded through the kitchen door. "Gran, where are you?"

I wonder if my teacher has called to ask Gran about giving a talk to my class on health and nutrition? And if she did, did Gran accept? I feel like Winnie the Pooh, 'Oh bother' I really have mixed feelings about her coming to talk to my class. On the one hand, I'm proud of all she's accomplished, but sometimes she goes on and on.

Gran came around the corner with a small armful of neatly folded clean clothes.

"Hi, Sweetheart, how was your day?"

"Pretty good. I got an 'A' on my statistics test." She hesitated, "Did my physiology teacher, Ms. Gobel, call you?"

"Yes, she did and I told her 'no'."

"You didn't!"

"No I didn't, but I sure wanted to."

"Afraid you'll get in trouble again?"

"Yes."

"I don't think you'll have to worry about the drug companies sic-ing the government on you this time. This is just a college class and not national television. And if you are that nervous about it then why did you agree?"

"Why do you think?"

"So you can improve the health of our nation's youth, or at least have a shot at doing so," Drew said.

Gran held her bundle of clothes tighter, put her fingers together and bowed, Charlie Chan style, and nodded, "Ah, so, number one son."

"You mean number one granddaughter."

"No, did you forget your cousin Lexi was born before you? You number *two* granddaughter." She bowed again then looked serious. "Now I just have to come up with an angle that will help them understand the correlation between real food and health, *and* make it interesting."

Drew stood still, her face unreadable.

"Well, are you just going to stand there? No great insight to share?"

"No, I'm going to study. If *I* have to listen to boring health lectures, why should my classmates get preferential treatment?"

"Are you insinuating that I'm boring?

"No, I'm stating unequivocally that you are boring."

Drew ducked and waited for something to come whizzing through the air at her. Nothing. No response. Had she hurt Gran's feelings? She looked up. Gran was staring at her intently.

"What are you thinking? Wait, you're not going to embarrass me in class are you?"

Gran shrugged with her arms still loaded with clean clothes, hence no free hands to throw something. "That's for me to know and you to worry about," Gran said as she walked around Drew and up the stairs. "By the way Drew thanks for the idea. Now let's see, what can I do to embarrass you? Hmm."

Chapter 9

Wednesday afternoon Gran walked down the hall of the Psychology building toward Miss. Gobel's office armed with 3x5 note cards and a basket of fruits, vegetables, and bunches of herbs.

She peered into office number 206. The woman at the desk appeared to be in her early forties. She looked up and smiled. "You must be Penny MacIntyre, Drew's grandmother. I'm really excited that you could make it. I've been looking forward to meeting you for a long time, even before I found out you were related to Drew."

"Well, I can't say I don't have reservations, but I think it's something I'm supposed to do."

The younger woman frowned. "There's one thing I need to warn you about. I've heard you're a Christian, and are rather vocal about it. I'm afraid that here on campus, religion is a taboo subject."

"I can't guarantee what I'll say. You'll either have to risk it or send me home." She reached over and slid her arm through her basket handle. "Just say the word and Little Red Riding Hood will take her basket and go skipping home; relieved to have an excuse not to face a room full of college students."

Miss Gobel hastened to stand up and grab the basket's handle. "No, don't be silly. I'll just answer any critics by saying that you got totally out of control and there was nothing I could do about it. Besides, if I have to face college students every day (with Drew being the worst) then I'm not letting you off the hook."

"Selfish, inconsiderate woman." Gran said.

Miss Gobel grinned.

As the bell rang, they entered the room together and the teacher introduced Gran to the class.

Gran was surprised how nervous she was. *OK, Lord, how about some help? Or I can stand here with my mouth hanging open for the next thirty minutes; your choice. . .*

She took a deep breath. "The human body is a marvelous creation. With proper care, it can last over one hundred years, and be fully functioning. Did anyone see the article about the ninety-seven-year old that won the 100-yard dash in the Senior Olympics? And, yes, he was really running. Your body *will* respond if you treat it right.

"New stem cell research has scientists believing our life span might reach 1000 years. When I say stem cells, I'm not talking about umbilical cord cells (which are great) or stem cells from unborn children (which are not great) but your own stem cells that act like a built in repair unit and last us our entire life-time. Stem cells decrease, as we get older. I have read several studies, which seem to prove that Klamath Lake, blue-green algae stimulates the production of stem cells. I'm assuming that other forms of greens and probiotics will be proved to improve production of stem cells as well.

"Stem cells are made in our bone marrow and can turn themselves into any kind of cell we need. For example, say one of your arteries is damaged, doctors can remove some of the artery cells, mix them with stem cells (after eight hours the stem cells become artery cells) and then inject them back into the damaged artery and they replace the damaged cells. Stem cells can transform into heart cells, knee joints, even teeth. Whenever an organ is in trouble it sends out a chemical message for help. When the cry for help enters the bloodstream, the stem cells rev-up and rush to rebuild. So why don't we live forever? Why do we have cancer, heart disease, etcetera? We don't have to. Most diseases, I believe, are self-imposed. Most of us don't understand how to eat right. We've all heard the catch phrase, 'When eating right and exercising is not enough?' Have you ever asked exactly what that means? I have. Many, scary to say, believe that five to seven servings of fruit and vegetables include ketchup (tomatoes-a vegetable), jam (a fruit), relish (a vegetable), and gummy bears (a fruit).

"The other factor, probably, the most important, is exercise. Walking a hilly neighborhood in the early morning is very good exercise *but* you can't stroll, you have to move out. You will never improve unless you push yourself. An active adult needs to walk 10,000 steps a day. Those people who only take 5000 steps are considered to be inactive adults and they can be subject to muscle and bone loss. If you have Alzheimer's, you can reduce the symptoms by fifty percent just by walking.

'Several years ago, I had a revelation about food in its original form and its relationship to the human body. I was looking through my vitamin catalogue and I happened to glance at the herb section, cinnamon, ginger, sage, dandelion, kudzu . . .kudzu? The weed that has taken over much of the South? What's that doing in a list of healing herbs? It seems there is something in Kudzu that helps reduce an alcoholic's craving for alcohol.

"And then it dawned on me. Everything that God created," She heard a sharp intake of breath, "He created for us. Every food was designed to mesh with the cellular structure of our body so that we would have perfect health. What happens when we fool around with the molecular structure of, say a soybean? Any ideas?"

"I'll bet it interferes with the body's utilization of the soybean." Wayne guessed, not waiting to be called on. "That's what all the controversy about genetically modified products is all about, isn't it. That's why a lot of soy breakfast drinks have a label proclaiming 'Non GMO'. Your body can't process genetically modified foods," Wayne said triumphantly.

"You are brilliant. We need more smart young people like you in leadership roles. Way to go. By the way, what's your name?" Gran asked.

Wayne looked stricken. He turned to Drew and mouthed, "Did you tell her what I said about her?"

Drew shook her head.

Gran asked, "What's going on?"

Wayne's face reddened.

"Wayne was under the mistaken belief that you staged the 'attack' for publicity purposes," Drew answered.

Gran looked at Wayne. "Wayne, if only you knew the amount of flack I'm getting from the government and the drug companies, you'd understand why publicity is the last thing I want or need right now."

She reached into her basket and withdrew a carrot and continued her presentation, "Foods are medicine. You've heard the common maxims; 'fish is brain food' or 'eat carrots to prevent night blindness'.

"Unfortunately, humans always think they can improve things. By using concentrated fertilizers, growers have created large, fast growing, *tasteless* produce. Not only is it tasteless but more importantly, it has less nutritional value. The nutritional value of non-organic food has dropped to fifteen percent of what it was in 1987.

"Anyone's brain feeling a little fuzzy?" Three students and Miss Gobel raised their hands. Gran reached into her basket and pinched off four sprigs of sage and two stalks of celery, which she broke in half and handed out. "Celery is also good for your skin.

"Immune system sluggish? Garlic and berries will do the trick." She set out the garlic and reached into her basket for her container of strawberries, raspberries and blueberries. "Garlic is a natural antibiotic and the raspberries were picked right out of my garden this morning. They are bursting with nutrients and flavor." As she opened the container, she noticed that something was very wrong. "Wait a minute; my raspberries are missing." She looked over at Drew and frowned.

Drew shrugged, "What can I say? Those were organic raspberries out of our garden, not the moldy tasteless berries from the store. No one could have resisted eating them."

"Which was to have been part of my demonstration. When did you get into my stuff? And did you have to eat every single one?"

"In answer to your first question, this morning, right after you picked them. In answer to your second question, yes."

"And you couldn't have gone out and picked your own?" Gran's voice sounded hurt.

"Couldn't. I would have been late for school. Besides, you were lucky I was able to restrain from eating the strawberries as well."

Gran hurriedly handed out the other berries; all the while giving Drew dirty looks. When she saw Drew sideling over toward the basket, she leaped in front of it.

"You touch those dark chocolate bars and you'll be sporting a cast for the next month."

Drew tried to edge around her. Gran could not remember ever being so angry with her granddaughter.

"No, you don't," Gran grabbed the two large chocolate bars and hugged them to her chest as she turned back to the students. She broke the still paper covered chocolate into chunks and quickly handed them out. Once all the chocolate was safely in the students' hand, Gran threw a smug smile at Drew who frowned and looked at Gran accusingly. "What kind of grandmother are you?"

"The best kind; the one that teaches you that there are consequences for your actions, whether it's stealing or eating the wrong foods.

"Dark Chocolate is one of the highest known sources of phenols, antioxidants, and oligamers, which clear the arteries of bad cholesterol build up."

Gran sounded upset s she continued, "We have a newsletter that comes out with some of the latest research. If you are interested in what foods help what conditions or if you would like to help us with the publication, I'm passing out a list. Please write down your e-mail address. Thank you for inviting me."

She felt like saying to Drew, "I hope you don't have much trouble finding a new place to live," but kept it to herself.

She loaded up her things while she waited for the list to come around, folded it, put it into her pocket, then said goodbye and left abruptly. She was so angry that she hadn't paid any attention as to how many had signed up. Tears threatened to run down her face. *How could that ungrateful child sabotage me like that? She knew I was nervous about giving this talk. Oh Lord, I failed you and them. I totally botched it.* She looked at all the stuff left in her basket that she hadn't mentioned, mushrooms now crushed, sliced apples turning brown. *Why would she do something like that?*

She ran down the steps to the back door that opened onto the teacher's parking lot where she'd been given special permission to park.

I thought we were going to be a team. She was supposed to be my ally; instead she sabotaged me. I feel betrayed.

"What a spoiled brat you are, Drew," Jon said disgustedly.

"How could you do something like that? She obviously worked hard on her presentation and to have her granddaughter, the one she was doing the presentation for, destroy the whole thing. I mean, whatever possessed you to eat her presentation?" Kevin added. "Besides, she had mushrooms in her basket and I would like to know what they are good for."

Drew didn't even look up from packing her backpack, "They are super immune system builders, especially Maitake and Shiitake mushrooms."

Kevin started to smile. "It was kind of funny; the looks she gave you. Hey, wait a minute. You did it on purpose. You wanted to make it funny, didn't you?"

"Yes, of course, it was supposed to be a joke. I didn't dream that she'd see it as betrayal. I have to stop her." She grabbed her backpack and took off at a run. She stopped short when she saw the empty parking spot. "Oh rats, I missed her." She retrieved her bike and rode back up the blacktop to her car.

Gran pulled into her driveway, pressed the garage door opener, and rushed into the house. She grabbed her soccer shoes and shorts and changed quickly.

On Wednesdays there was usually a scrimmage game at the park for all the die-hard soccer players. Whoever showed up could play. Gran liked the variety of people, the variety of ages (fifteen to seventy five), and the variety of skills. The great thing about it, besides giving her another day to run, was that she could play hard as she could or not. With her scheduled games, she had to pace her self because there usually were no women subs. *The way I feel right now, I'm going to run like crazy and take my aggression out on the ball.*

She pulled into the parking lot above the field. She was still angry. Before she flung the car door open, it occurred to her that the feeling flowing through her was pain and humiliation. She felt hurt. Drew had deliberately betrayed and sabotaged her. Tears started to waterfall down her face as she crossed her arms over the steering wheel and put her head on them and sobbed. *Drew hates me. I failed. I failed to get them to understand and I made a fool of myself in the process.*

Before she totally lost it, she became aware of a figure standing outside of her car window. She looked up. *Oh, it's Jim. How embarrassing.* She turned the ignition on and opened the window. "Hi."

"What's going on? Are you OK?" Concern marked his handsome face. Jim was one of the regular soccer players. Gran had been playing soccer with him for twenty years. He had just turned fifty but looked much younger. He was the kind of man who cared about other people and remembered special days like birthdays and anniversaries.

"Come and walk with me to the field and you can tell me what's so upsetting."

As they descended the hill and started across field two, Gran told him about her botched health presentation to Drew's class and about Drew's sabotage.

"Are you sure she did it deliberately?"

"Well, making her grandmother look like a scatterbrained idiot, took *some* forethought.

Granted, she probably didn't have to stay up all night planning it, but it did take *some* planning."

"You don't buy the 'couldn't resist the raspberries' story?"

Gran rolled her eyes. "Right."

Jim noticed a very attractive young woman with a reddish-brown ponytail bolting down the hill.

"If I'm not mistaken, I think we're about to find out. Is the granddaughter we're talking about the same one who's being recruited by the women's Olympic soccer team?"

Gran nodded as she looked back up the hill and cringed.

"I don't think I can face her."

"Sure you can. I'll protect you," Jim said as he put his arm on her shoulder.

If the sight of a strange man with his arm around her grandmother bothered her, you would never know it. Drew was on a mission and nothing was going to interfere. She pulled up short in front of them, not even a little out of breath, plucked Jim's arm off Gran's shoulder and pulled Gran into her arms. For a long moment, nothing was said.

Finally Drew swallowed and said, "It was supposed to be a joke."

Gran looked thoughtful. After a few moments she said, "I was telling Jim how talented you were and how there is nothing you can't do. I have now found something you suck at."

"Making jokes?"

"You got it."

Chapter 10

Papa had a Sunday morning routine. He got up early, checked his e-mail, and then got everybody else up to get ready for church. He always liked to 'get a jump on the day' so they went to the eight o'clock service. The drive to church took exactly fifteen minutes so Papa would remind people how much time they had. Then he would say, "I'll be out in the car." If the others failed to appear, he would honk the horn. This morning there were no reminders; Papa sat in the rocking chair by the kitchen window reading the newspaper. Gran came downstairs to put on her contacts. She came out of the bathroom and looked over at Papa.

"What's going on? We'll be late," she said.

"I don't like that song," Papa said

"What song?" Gran asked.

"That awful song they sing every Sunday during Lent. It's called 'litany' or something like that."

"You know, John . . ."

"Yes, I know him well," Papa finished for her. Gran was going to say, "You know John, you're being rather silly, don't you think?" but

gave up and said instead, "Come on, let's go."
She headed for the door. Drew and Bob were
coming down the stairs.

"Aren't we going to be late?" Bob asked.

"Not if we leave right now," Gran said, as
she climbed into the front passenger seat of the
Buick.

"Late is good," Drew mumbled. She didn't
like church. She thought it was a waste of time,
but she knew it made Gran and Papa happy.
They got in the car and headed out.

Papa was acting strange today. He didn't
complain once about red lights. He seemed glad
when people were slow in starting when the light
changed. When they got to the church parking
lot, he drove at a snail's pace all the way
through the lot and into the overflow lot. Finally,
Gran said, "For Pete's sake, park the car. What
in the world is wrong with you?" Then she
remembered his comment about the song.
"You're not serious about the song, are you?"

He nodded sheepishly.

"Well, it is long and the words are strange
in places," she agreed. "So you've been stalling
so that we'd miss a song?"

He nodded.

As they entered the courtyard, they saw that the foyer was still filled with people. Gran let out a hoot of laughter. The priest wasn't there yet. Father Brian had overslept. The song hadn't been sung yet. All Papa's effort had been wasted. They had a very disgruntled Papa on their hands. He thought he was being so clever. Gran told all their friends about why they were late. Some laughed, but a lot of them, especially the men, said. "Yeah, we hate that song too."

"Well, you can't say God doesn't have a sense of humor," Gran grinned. "Sometimes he has to let us know that we're not the ones in control, no matter how much we'd like to be," she said, as she looked meaningfully at Papa and Drew

A tall thin man carrying the cross led the procession down the aisle to the front of the church. Behind him came a deacon, two alter servers and finally, the associate pastor, Father Bryan, a tall, good-looking man with curly blond hair.

As he approached the altar, small children gathered in excited anticipation. When Father

Bryan entered the open area between the pews and the wide steps to the altar, the children rushed in to give the priest 'high fives'; then smiling at their accomplished feat of daring, they drifted back to their seats. Father Bryan smiled at the children's delight but looked like he would have enjoyed another hour in bed.

The 'big man' was Monsignor Bishop and, although he was almost a foot shorter than Father Bryan, was the boss and oversaw the schedule. He usually tried to avoid the eight o'clock mass.

It was he who had started the 'high fives'. His love for children was evident as he hugged, smiled and nose tweaked his way through the crowds of people that constituted his congregation. Maybe, as he once remarked, he related well to children because, like them, he was a short person in a tall world. When he first came to the parish, he had replaced a gentle giant of a man and had been forced to buy a new priest's chair because it was hard to be dignified when your feet dangled a foot from the floor. With boyish good looks, intelligence, and a well-developed sense of humor, he ruled his parish with a gentle but firm hand. And since he was the 'big man', he was not celebrating this early service.

Father Bryan stepped up on the platform, walked to the back of the altar and sat down in the center chair. Drew wondered how comfortable the little chair was for Father Bryan. Father Bryan stood up almost immediately and walked back towards the congregation. As he looked out at the parishioners, a grin spread across his face. "I have to tell you what happened to Monsignor."

He adjusted his mike and walked back and forth in front of the congregation.

"You all know how Monsignor hates to fly. He has an irrational fear of planes. Once he's airborne, he's fine, but making himself get on a plane and stay on the plane often requires Herculean efforts. Usually he has to get a few drinks under his belt in order to control his fear. Last week, he and some of the church staff had to fly to a conference. Monsignor got himself on the plane and buckled into his seat. He was trying to keep himself from thinking about all the crashes that occur at takeoff. Just then,

Marilyn, his secretary, said she thought she smelled an overheated iron. Monsignor didn't smell anything. Suddenly a voice came over the speakers telling them to stay calm and to quietly exit the plane. *One of the engines was on fire.* It was all monsignor could do not to leap up and run down the aisle, pushing all others out of the way, while screaming 'Let the priest go first, let the priest go first.' Fortunately, he was able to comport himself with dignity.

"Eventually they were put on a different plane. Whereas before, no one had paid any attention to Monsignor's Roman collar, now everyone wanted to sit by 'the priest', be blessed by the priest, or at least touch the priest."

"Monsignor asked the flight attendant if he could try to make the passengers more at ease. She told him to do whatever he could. I think she was thinking more along the lines of prayer and counseling. Instead he went up to each row of people and said, with a straight face, 'Would you like a prayer cloth? I don't have them with me, but if you'll give me your credit card number and address, I'll send one to you.' Some people looked at him like he was crazy; some started to take out their wallets, and some realized that it was a joke and hooted with laughter. Can't you just see him doing that?"

Drew found herself grinning as she looked at the faces around her. There were a few who shook their heads, but the majority was laughing. A few were nodding; they were the ones, she thought, who realized that in order to be able to do that, Monsignor had to have overcome his fear. They seemed proud of him. Drew was proud of him, too.

On the way to the car, Drew decided to bait Gran, "Well, Gran, wasn't that great that Monsignor was able to overcome his fear all by himself?"

"Yes, that was great." Gran replied, trying not to smile.

"Wait a minute; aren't you going to say that God should get all the credit?" Drew asked

"That goes without saying," Gran said

"Doesn't anyone ever get any credit for accomplishments besides God?"

"Drew, it's not a contest between you and God," Gran said as she put her arm around Drew, "It's a team effort."

Chapter 11

Drew and Bob woke up early the next morning. Bob lay in bed as Drew sat on the edge of the bed with her long legs hanging over the side.

"You know, Bob, I..."

"Yes, I know him well," Bob said. He looked over at Drew, waiting for her reaction. At first she glared at him through frowning eyebrows, and then she shrieked, threw her hands up in the air and fell back onto the bed.

"Oh no, I married Papa." Her voice was muffled because her hands covered her mouth. She rolled over onto her elbows and inched her way toward his face.

Bob reached down and pulled her up onto his stomach.

"So you're saying that all great male minds think alike?" He grinned as he looked into her laughing blue eyes.

"I'm saying you interrupted my great thought, which for the moment, I can't remember. Now you just have to take my word for it. It was very deep."

"So deep you can't remember it?" he asked.

"Yeah, that just about sums it up."

She slipped her arms around his neck and leaned closer.

"Are you leaning?" he asked

"Un–huh," she waited a moment. "Are you going to kiss me?"

"Un–huh." he mumbled as he closed the distance between them and kissed her.

By the time they got downstairs, the whine of the chain saw was almost deafening.

They were surprised Gran had been able to get Papa to wait until the neighbors were awake before he started cutting.

The Bradford pear trees, which had been so beautiful, were now overgrown. Even though Papa and Gran had tried to keep them pruned; the last windstorm had caused them to split. Now the trees were in a twisted mass. Gran was outside supervising the cutting into four-foot lengths. Sometimes Papa was a little accident prone, so on potentially dangerous projects Gran liked to be out there with him, just in case.

Drew looked out the narrow paned window on one side of the door, and Bob watched from the other side.

"Do you think we'll do as well as they have?" Drew asked.

"Absolutely," Bob answered.

"How can you be so sure?"

"Because family and commitment are important to both of us. You have to want it bad enough to fight for it. And I picked a real scrapper."

Drew turned toward Bob and put her fists up in fighting position; she brushed her thumbs against the side of her nose and bounced back and forth in front of him, making pretend jabs at him. "That's me, the Mad Scrapper."

Just then the door flew open and Gran came bursting through the door.

"Oh Bob, glad you're up. I need your muscles out there. That tree trunk is too heavy for me." She turned to look at Drew. "Was that a new dance you were doing, Drew?"

Drew grinned at Bob, "Yeah, something like that. It's called 'Let's do the scrap.'"

"Oh, really? That sounds like fun!" Gran said. "Maybe when we have more time, you can teach me."

Chapter 12

Drew's statistics teacher, Dr. Evans, was a loose-limbed, 48-year-old man with gray sprinkled hair. Drew liked him immensely. Although he was an intellectual, he genuinely liked people, especially his students. Today their discussion had gotten off statistics and wandered into spiritual speculation.

"Well, we all know that prayer doesn't work." Dr. Evans stated.

"How do we know that?" Drew asked. She was immediately intrigued, because she was always disagreeing with Gran about God. Drew never doubted that there was a Creator, because the probability of the world and its life forms evolving from light and chemicals, in her view, was zero. However, the personal God of Gran's who was concerned with lost CD's or parking spots eluded her.

"People over the centuries have said 'God save the King' and kings have the shortest life spans of all."

Drew waited expectantly for him to go on. Finally she realized that there would be no further observation.

Drew whooped, "What? That's it? You're kidding, right?"

Dr. Evans's long pleasant face lengthened even more as his jaw dropped and his eyebrows rose. He had made that observation for years, and no one had ever responded like this. Several people had disagreed quietly about prayer, but he had squelched them because he said there was no documentation and their arguments were all subjective. He enjoyed Drew as a student. She was very bright and she had a delightful sense of humor. He was curious as to what she had to say.

"I *thought* I was serious. What are your thoughts?" he asked.

"Well, although I'm not an expert on God, I do know that saying 'God save the King' is not a prayer. I think it's more akin to 'Heil Hitler' than a prayer. A prayer is communication between you and your creator. Its effects have been documented. In the July 1988 issue of *Southern Medical Journal,* in an article pertaining to patient healing, Dr. Randolph Byrd found that there was an 8% improvement over the control group and there may have been a greater difference because they did not know if any members of the control group had been prayed for. Then there is Duke University's Harold Koenig, who has released the book, *Handbook of Religion and Health* which includes 1,200 studies . . ."

"OK, stop! I concede."

"You capitulated after one statistic?"

He looked over at Drew. "Richardson, I've had you in several classes, and I can tell by the 'lecture' tone in your voice that you have researched this subject thoroughly. This will teach me to come to a conclusion without checking the facts. Next class, we will deal with statistical significance. I hope you be as prepared for that issue as you were for me. I can't believe you ruined my great premise," he jokingly complained.

Just before the bell rang, Drew said, 'God save the Queen' seemed to work for the queens, Elizabeth, Victoria, and the current Elizabeth.

Maybe that means God likes women better," Drew said as the students began to file out.

Dr. Evans made a Frankenstein face, held his arms out in front and pivoted in her direction.

"Urrrrr," he growled as he approached her.

"Eeeeek," she shrieked in mock horror, grabbed her books, papers and backpack, and ran toward the door.

Dr. Hull, the Dean of the department, came out of his office just in time to almost collide with 'Frankenstein' as he lurched through the doorway.

"Dr. Evans, you are an excellent teacher but you need to set a better example in deportment. May I remind you that if you wish to be treated with respect, you need to behave with more dignity? You know that we are making inroads into getting Psychology accepted as a bona fide science. Your behavior is not helping our cause. Do we have an understanding?" Dr. Hull demanded.

"Yes Sir, we do."

"Somehow, you don't look very contrite," Dr. Hull said.

"Oh, but I am contrite, Sir. Would you like me to salute, Sir?"

"That won't be necessary." The Dean wagged his head as he walked back into his office.

Chapter 13

Gran was sitting at the kitchen table writing when Drew got home.

"Greetings, Grandchild, how was school?"

Drew ran Gran a play-by-play. She even acted out Dr. Evans's impersonation. Gran laughed, "Drew, you are a wonderful impressionist. How about editing my column?"

"How did we get from a good impressionist to editing your column?" Drew asked.

"We went from *wonderful* impressionist to *wonderful* editor. I thought if I gave you compliment, you'd be more likely to help me. How about it?"

"Sure, I'm on a roll." She took a sheet of paper from Gran, walked into the den and threw herself into one of the dark green overstuffed chairs. She kicked off her shoes and put her feet on the hassock and leaned back. The column was only a page, so she made short work of editing. She came through the double doors and into the kitchen hallway.

"Gran, this is great. I love it. Is it true that a bowl of organic carrots is the cutting edge of cancer prevention? But, you might want to say 'nature' instead of 'God'. God tends to turn off some people."

"Drew, all I seem to do lately is turn people off. The truth is supposed to set you free, but all it seems to do for me lately is get me into hot water. Besides, I prayed before I wrote it, and that would be like slapping God in the face. Here He gives me the story and the words, and then I deny him the credit. What kind of gratitude is that?"

Drew felt the anger starting to rise within her.

"Why do you always give God the credit? You wrote this. It's good because of your talent. God didn't have anything to do with it."

"Drew, who gave me the talent? The opportunity?" She asked as she looked at the angry set of Drew' face. "Drew," Gran said firmly, "If I deny Him before man, He will deny me before God. I will not deny my God, Drew, not even for you." She took the paper from Drew's hands and turned to go.

Drew put her hand on Gran's arm and said in an imploring voice, "But Gran, I can't believe like you. I want to, I really do, but I can't."

Gran stopped and turned back to her granddaughter. She brushed Drew's red-gold hair away from her face and looked up into her tear filled eyes, "Drew, Jesus is real. God is real. You either want Him in your life, or you don't. You make the choice."

"But I've tried." Drew said.

"You get on your knees and ask him into your life. He won't come unless you ask. Then expect him to move. Drew, Honey, Jesus loves you so much." She put her arms around her. She sighed. "Drew, people like you, who are super competent, often have a difficult time asking for help because they can do everything. Look at you. You're smart, you're a super athlete, you play the piano, you sing, act, and draw. There's nothing you can't do well, even brilliantly. Sometimes that can be a curse, because you don't ever need help. But Drew, there will come a time when things will be out of your control, and you *will* need God's help. If you ask Him, He will come and be with you. If you seek Him, you will find Him."

They stood in the hallway and held each other. Not counting the raspberry affair (a misunderstanding), this was their first argument in years because they were usually able to discuss things. Drew didn't understand, and Gran didn't know how to explain the invisible spiritual world that even at this instant swirled around them.

Chapter 14

Gran looked at the jeep's clock, almost 7:30 on a Tuesday night, prayer group night. It was a beautiful spring evening. Dogwoods and azaleas were putting on a show, each one trying to outdo the other. Gran didn't really notice. Michael W. Smith was singing her favorite worship songs on the radio. Her lips didn't move. Her mind was on Drew. How she loved that child, but how to make her understand that God was real?

Gran remembered the joy she had felt the first time she had come to the prayer group. She finally found a place where she could talk about God and praise God, out loud, and be perfectly accepted. If she said anything at home, people would either jump on her words or roll their eyes. At prayer group she could praise to her heart's content.

"Lord, if there's something you need me to do, please let me know. If there is something you want me to say, tell me."

She drove into the driveway and parked about six spaces up under the trees. She pulled her new purse over her shoulder and picked up her Bible with its cloth-covered case. She liked it because of the cloth handle on the back, which made it easier to carry, and she could keep her little book of daily readings inside it. She gathered her stuff, then slammed the door of the Jeep with her knee. She didn't lock it, because if she did lock it, the Jeep had been known to sound the alarm even when not disturbed.

She liked to walk along the path through the park-like setting that wound behind the church. She noticed a man standing by the back emergency exit, smoking. She nodded and proceeded up the path. His presence cast a pall on the peace she usually felt walking through the landscaped grounds. Reaching the front of the church, she pulled the door open into the chapel. There were about fifteen people sitting in chairs or putting out the songbooks. They all smiled and gave her a warm welcome. Most of them rose and came over to hug her. It felt good to have warm, loving, accepting arms surrounding her. She felt completely safe and sheltered.

I'm home, she thought. The hour and a half flew by. She sang and prayed and let God's love and spirit flow through her like a river flows over and around every nook and cranny within its boundaries.

Luxuriating in the spirit's presence, she was one of the last to leave. She walked out of the chapel and started down the path. It was much darker now. The subdued landscape lights only seemed to cast deeper shadows. She heard a rustle that told her that someone was standing on the far side of the shrubbery by the high brick wall. She continued away from the sound, through the shadows toward the streetlight.

The man was still smoking by the exit. Gran notice the pile of cigarette butts that had accumulated at his feet.

He must be a chain smoker, she thought. When she came even with him, he stepped toward her. He made no effort to hide the hunting knife he pulled from the sheath on his belt. She looked back up the path. Another man stood there blocking the way back to light and safety. The smoker lunged at her with his knife. Instinctively, Gran backhanded him with her Bible. The knife flew out of his hand. The man grunted and stooped to pick up his knife. Gran knew she had made him angry. She took a deep breath, clutched her Bible to her chest, and sprinted down the driveway, across the street and up the steep hill on the other side.

"Run her down, Sam!" The man near the wall yelled.

They want me to run. They know about my heart. She could feel fear start to invade her mind, and then it faded.

"If I can't outrun a cigarette addict, I deserve to die. Okay Lord, I need some help here," she whispered.

Normally she would need to warm up by running the length of the soccer field before she undertook a grueling uphill run, but today she ran up the hill effortlessly. She wasn't even slightly winded as she neared the top of the hill.

Hearing a cry behind her, she looked back down the hill. About a third of the way up, her would-be attacker was on his hands and knees. His labored breathing could be easily heard.

"Bud, help, I can't breathe," he gasped.

The other man was crossing the street. "Blast it, Sam, you told me you were a track star in high school." Bud grumbled as he stomped up to his companion. "How bad are you?" He yanked him to his feet.

"I can't breathe. I think I'm having a heart attack."

"You've got to be kidding. Forget the heart attack. There's no way I'm taking you to the emergency room."

"But I can't breathe."

Gran ran through the yards and back toward the street. She was careful to keep down and out of sight. She would try to circle back to her Jeep, and then call the police. The bad thing about her plan was that when she reached the road, she would be out in the open and the other guy, Bud; she thought that was his name, might be in better shape. *Wait a minute; I still have my new purse clutched under my arm and what do I have in my new purse? My cell phone.* She pulled it out and called 911. She pushed through the bushes and around the fences until she got to the road. She saw that 'Bud' had brought the car over to where Sam had collapsed. The front door of the car was open and 'Bud' had his hands on Sam's lower back as he struggled to push Sam into the front seat. He finally got him into the car and closed the door.

Gran aimed her cell phone at the car and took a picture because she was hopeless when it came to car makes and models. Unless the vehicle was a Jeep, GM truck, a Buick, or a Maxima like Drew's, they all looked the same to her. She could hear Bud cursing and yelling at the poor hapless Sam. *Hey wait a minute; he tried to kill me; why am I feeling sorry for him?*

She took a chance and crouched as she ran across the street into the bushes on the other side. From here she could read the first three letters of the license plate, which she read off to the police operator. She told the officer in which direction Sam and Bud were headed as she watched them back out and roar down the street into the darkness. She sighed and went back up the path to the church's emergency exit and knelt near the cigarette pile. She scooped up some of the non-smoldering cigarette butts into a piece of paper, which she folded into an envelope. She waited for the police car to arrive.

The policeman finally showed up. She told them about the attack on Drew and that she thought that it was the same two men.

She retraced her steps for the police officers then pointed to the back entrance to the church and the pile of cigarette butts.

"Captain Greg Richardson is working on the previous attacks. I was going to give you these cigarette butts, however the more I think about it, I more I realize that I need to leave the investigation to you. I took them from that pile over there."

The officer looked over at the cigarettes on the ground, reached for her envelope, pulled a small camera out of his pocket, and took some pictures.

"I always carry it with me, just in case. We don't bring a tech person out on routine matters."

"Routine matters? Someone tries to kill me and you call it routine? Just because they were inept doesn't mean that they didn't try to kill me. I was feeling invigorated about thwarting their attempt. I thought you might say, 'Great job,' but I guess not, since it was a *routine matter,* and since it was only a *routine matter,* I won't give you my cell phone. But I will let you look at the pictures I took of the car.

"And I will come to the police station in the morning and you can have the two pictures I took." She pulled up the pictures on her phone and held it out to him. He and the other officer looked at the pictures and immediately identified the car make and model. They called it in.

"Mrs. MacIntyre, would you recognize the two men?"

She looked at him and bit her lip.

The interrogating officer grinned, "You're debating whether to give me a smart alecky comment or a simple 'yes', aren't you?"

"Yes." Now it was her turn to grin.

"OK, you can go. But try to stay out of trouble. By the way, I enjoy your column." He grinned back at her.

She was still grinning when she got into the Jeep.

"He wasn't so bad after all. At least he has good taste in newspaper columns.

"I should be a nervous wreck. A man threatened me with a knife. And I hit him with my Bible, that strap on the case really came in handy. But I don't think that's what they had in mind when they said that the word of God is a mighty weapon. They wanted to kill me, yet here I am driving home feeling very pleased with both God and myself.

"By the way, Lord, good job. I flew up that hill; I wish you'd help me run like that on the soccer field. I'd be in the Olympics. I even ran in loafers carrying a purse and a Bible. Lord, I'm impressed. You made me run like a gazelle."

She turned up the volume on the CD player and sang at the top of her lungs, praising God, and she meant every word of it.

When she got home, she saw that everyone else was already there. Cocoa, Papa's chocolate-point Siamese cat greeted her with his deep "meow" as she opened the Jeep door and climbed out. She snuck in the back way so no one would notice how late she was. Cocoa ran in front of her and, for some strange reason, known only to him, he threw himself on the step in front of her and rolled to his back. Gran, familiar with his strange ritual, managed to avoid stepping on him. "Cocoa, why do you insist on doing the Fosbury flop? Oh, you don't know about the Fosbury Flop? Well, long before you were born," she gathered him into her arms and sat on the carpeted back steps, "during the Olympics, in 1968, I think, a young man with the last name Fosbury, changed high jumping forever. Instead of kicking one leg up in a scissor motion, he flung himself over the bar, face up.

"I spent hours in the back yard practicing the high jump for the school Olympics, but I never had the nerve to fling myself into space. Now that I think about it, all I had to do was haul out a mattress to land on." She turned Cocoa's whiskered face toward hers, leaned close and rubbed noses. "Just think; I might have become a world famous high jumper, Penny Walters and her mattress. Instead, I'm Penny MacIntyre, heath lady"

Cocoa gave her a peculiar look, rose, stretched, jumped out of her arms and continued up the stairs. His facial expression looked like he was thinking, "The things I have to put up with for a lousy back scratch."

Chapter 16

Bud kept his word and did not take Sam to the emergency room.

"I can't believe how pathetic you are, pathetic and stupid. Everyone knows that you can't chain smoke and still run. I don't know how my wife could have such a loser for a brother. Oh, the big track star; heck, you barely made it across the street. _I_ could have done a better job. A seventy-five-year-old lady left you in the dust. Boy, do I know how to pick 'em. What a loser." He was working himself into frenzy. "A loooser" He dragged the word out and made the 'L' sign on his forehead. He repeated the loser sign and ended up pointing at his brother-in-law. "Loser."

"You already said that. Now shut up. She's not any seventy-five. That woman ran like a deer or one of those African cantaloupes."

"Cantaloupe?" Bud shouted, "An African cantaloupe? You idiot. It's an antelope." He shook his head. "I don't believe it. No one could be that stupid. Why me?"

"I meant antelope," Sam said petulantly.

"You did not."

The car slowed and Sam realized that they were at the spot where they had stolen the car.

"Get out." Bud yelled. Although Sam got out very slowly, he seemed to be feeling better.

"It must have been a false alarm. I'm feeling much better," Sam said.

Bud wiped the car down with a rag as best he could to get rid of the fingerprints. He had worn gloves, but his idiot brother-in-law had taken his off when he was smoking. When he finished, he got out and walked over to his car, which was parked out of sight around the corner. They both climbed in and drove off with Bud still grumbling.

Chapter 16

Gran was in Greg's office first thing the next morning. She hadn't told anybody about her evening because she felt sure that between the evidence from Drew's encounter and hers, that the case would be wrapped up very quickly. She didn't tell Papa because she knew he'd start yelling at her for not being more careful. He always yelled when he felt helpless. She knew why he did it but she still didn't like to be the object of his frustration.

"All's well that ends well," she said. "I'll tell them later when we have the bad guys safely in jail."

Greg had the officer's report in his hand. He didn't need the pictures of the car because the officers had found it. They also discovered that it must have been stolen, although the owner hadn't been aware that it had been missing. They weren't real successful with fingerprints either, but the cigarettes might prove useful if and when they found the suspects. There were prints on the cigarettes, which they were comparing with the prints on the Jeep. They did take Gran's phone, because although the pictures were taken at a distance, the two men should be recognizable.

A police artist was brought in, and Gran described the men.

Chapter 17

Drew came to Dr Evans' statistics class dressed in soccer shorts and a T-shirt. Soccer practice was scheduled right after class and she was looking forward to it. She loved her coach.

She tossed her ponytail over her shoulder as she sat down, deposited her backpack on the floor beside her, and then rummaged through it for a pencil. She heard a sniff and looked in the direction of the sound.

Karen, one of her classmates, her dark hair cut short around her face, had red swollen eyes. She clutched a Kleenex in her hand.

"Karen, what's wrong?" Drew asked. More sniffing. Drew knew Karen was pregnant. She had known Karen for three years. Karen and her husband, Bob had been trying to have children. So far, Karen had two miscarriages. They had been very hopeful about this pregnancy.

"It's not the baby, is it?" One look at Karen's bereft face answered her question.

"Oh, Karen, I'm so sorry."

"Bob says we're through trying. It's too emotionally draining. He says we can look into adopting. I wanted this baby so bad. I could feel him moving inside me." She started sobbing. Drew got up and came around the table, but Karen shook her head and held her hand up to keep Drew where she was. Drew knew she and Karen would totally break down if she even touched Karen. Drew sat back down.

"Did you try the vitamin E? The real vitamin E, not the synthetic?"

"No, we don't believe in that all of that stuff."

Anger flashed through Drew. "So rather than try something natural that works, you keep killing your babies because you *don't believe* in all that stuff? Are you stupid?"

Drew watched in horror as Karen dissolved before her eyes. She moved like her brain was short-circuiting. She'd start to move her head right, stop, and shake slightly. Her hand clutched at the table edge.

"Oh, my God, Karen, I didn't mean that. Please forgive me." She rushed around the table and knelt beside Karen. She tried to put her arms around her. Karen took Drew's hand and pushed it off her arm.

"Don't touch me." She slowly pushed her chair out and stood up. Drew rose and moved aside.

"Please let me help you." Drew pleaded.

Karen looked at her with derision.

"I think you have done enough." She walked shakily out of the room. Drew started to go after her. A hand on her arm stopped her. Drew looked around. The hand belonged to Becky, one of their tablemates. She was a small blonde woman whose glare sent shivers down Drew's spine.

"She's right. You have done enough. Nothing like kicking someone when they're down." Drew stepped back and let Becky by. "I'll make sure nothing else happens to her." Becky said as she started after Karen.

Why did I say such a horrible thing? Because I was irritated that Karen hadn't taken my advice? No, that wasn't it at all. I really care about Karen, and I hate to see her hurting. So then what did I do? I hurt her so badly; she may never recover.

Am I like that parent I saw in the park? The man had been pushing his two-year-old daughter in a swing and the little girl had fallen off and hurt herself. The father rushed to her, yelling, "I told you to be careful. How could you be so stupid?"

Drew thought the man was angry with the child but he was really mourning the fact that his child had been hurt.

When she became aware of her surroundings, class was proceeding. Dr. Evans was writing equations on the green blackboard. He was lecturing, and Drew had not written down one word. She let his voice float over her and sooth her. It was a nice voice.

You know, I'm really not a mean person. She thought, *in fact, I'm usually a very nice person.*

"Penny for your thoughts." The nice voice broke through her thoughts. She looked up with a start. The classroom was deserted except for her and her teacher.

"What happened?" he asked.

"I'd rather not talk about it," she said.

"Be that as it may, you need to start at the beginning."

She gave him a wry look. She reluctantly told him. He was quiet as he digested the information. "It hurt you to see her suffer so you did some research when she first miscarried."

"Asked Gran."

"And not only didn't Karen try it, she threw it back in your face. And because she didn't try it, she made you watch her suffer all over again."

Drew looked across at his sweet face.

"You are such a nice man."

"Sometimes," he laughed. "Oh, I have another question for you. You were crying in class today, and I know my lecture wasn't *that* bad."

Drew looked thoughtful, then graced him with a smile.

"No, it had nothing to do with your lecture. I guess I was mourning for Karen's baby. I was also thinking about something my grandmother always harps about. When my cousin and I were small, we were terrible eaters. My cousin was the worst (she still is), because she hated fruits and vegetables. She didn't like the texture. My grandmother had convulsions over her eating habits. She'd try to help us understand how important eating right was. She'd say, 'Your cells are trying to build you the best bodies in the world. How can you become tall and strong if you never give your bodies anything to work with? "Pretend you're a general in an army. Your job is to build a strong wall to protect your troops from invasion. You start looking for things to build a strong wall with, but all you can find to build with are crushed pop cans, chip packages, and candy bar wrappers. What kind of wall would that be?'

"We just laughed. What did it matter what we ate? We were young and there didn't seem to be any consequences. Gran was just being obsessive with all this hoopla about what we ate. But when I was sitting here looking at the candy bar wrappers and chip packages that Karen left, I got this image of her tiny baby trying so hard to grow and build his little body into a strong and healthy body. And all the poor little guy had to work with was garbage." Tears started down her face, "There is not one thing in that whole pile of

114

junk for that baby to grow with. Then she was going to top it off with a toxic diet drink. He was trying so hard, little hands moving and little feet kicking." Drew started sobbing for the little person who hadn't the strength to continue his struggle for life and had lost his fragile hold.

Dr. Evans patted Drew's shoulder because he didn't know what else to do.

The dean of the department looked into the open doorway. Dr. Evans looked up and quickly brushed his tears away with the palm of his hand.

Drew started laughing and crying.

"It's going to be all right." Dr. Evans said.

"Dr. Evans, what the devil is going on?" asked the dean.

"The worst seems to be over. I think we're coming down the home stretch," Dr. Evans said.

He turned to Drew, "Don't you have soccer practice? You can pretend you're the soccer ball and kick yourself until you feel better."

When she looked up at him, he could see the tears still glistening on her long dark lashes. He wanted to put his arms around her like he did when his little daughter, Hannah, cried. He knew that was out of the question. He was in enough trouble for his Frankenstein act.

."Go on, Richardson, you'll be late." He said instead.

Drew got up, gave him a subdued smile, and forced herself to leave the classroom.

The dean came in and sat down across from Dr. Evans.

"That your lunch?" He pointed at the stuff Karen had left. "If it is, I can't see how you can eat like that and still keep your boyish figure."

Dr. Evans looked down at the junk beside him. He picked up the wrappers and the torn bag of chips and tossed them into the garbage. He threw away the unopened soda can as well. Still staring at the trashcan, he said. "I wonder how they keep that stuff from eating through the can."

The dean waited for Evans to turn his attention back to him.

"Can you tell me why most of the females in your class exited en masse before the class even began?"

Dr. Evans told him what he knew. When he finished, the dean sighed. His prematurely white hair looked tousled and his hazel eyes looked tired.

"Bob, do I need to remind you again? We work very hard to give psychology its rightful place in academia as a science. But what do we get? Sobbing women, teachers acting like Frankenstein, and now that same teacher is wiping tears from his eyes. Are you single-handedly trying to destroy all that we've worked for?"

Now was Dr. Evan's turn to sigh and shake his head.

"Drew, er, *Miss, no, she's married, Mrs.* Richardson," he corrected, sensing the dean's censure, "said she had this image of Karen's tiny baby fighting for life against impossible odds, trying to grow big and strong on junk food and losing the battle in the end. I thought about my kids when they were babies, how they would grab the end my finger in their little hands. It made me feel very protective of them. But this little guy that Drew described broke my heart. I don't know if poor nutrition killed him. I'm sure lots of kids survive eating junk food." He frowned, and then continued, "Drew says her grandmother thinks that junk food proves that God exists. According to her, if we fed dogs what we feed our children, the dogs would be dead in three weeks.

"You know," Evans continued, "Marcia and I lost a child between Bob, my oldest child, and Hannah my youngest child. It was pretty traumatic. So I guess that's why Drew's comments struck so close to home.

"By the way, I thought you had a meeting with the board of directors today. How did you hear about the exodus?"

"Karen? Is that her name? I keep confusing her with Melanie Talbot; they both have similar builds and short black hair. I know they really don't look alike, but I never can remember who is who. Anyway, she was almost hysterical; kept yelling that she wanted to talk to Bob. I left a meeting in my office, thinking she was yelling about you. It turns out she wanted her husband, Bob. I finally figured it out when I asked her if she wanted me to get you, and she kept saying, "I want my Bob, not your Bob."

A look of comprehension crossed Dr Evans's face. "My Bob? Oh, now I understand.

Now it makes sense. Karen's husband is named Bob. Drew's husband must also be named Bob. She always refers to him as 'my Bob.' I thought she must be married to some foreign guy, 'My Bob', but she wasn't, she was just clarifying which Bob they were talking about. Boy, we have Bobs all over the place. Although you are a Bill and not a Bob, you have a son named Bob, I'm Bob and I have a son named Bob." Sensing a swing from maudlin to giddiness, Dr. Hull tried to forestall it.

"Why don't you take off early?" he asked hopefully.

"I'm OK. I have a guidance appointment in ten minutes, but thanks. You just don't want me to start in on Bob jokes."

Bill smiled, "that about sums it up."

"Here a Bob, there a Bob."

"Get out of here, or better yet," he pointed toward Bob's office, "go to your room."

Bob grinned and stood up.

"Thanks, Bill, I needed that."

Dr. Hull relaxed. *Good, for the moment I have averted a repeat of the dignity loss of several days ago.* A moment later he cringed as he heard Bob's high tenor voice fill the hallway.

"Bob, Bob, Bob, Bob Barber Ann, Bob, Bob, Bob, Bob Barber Ann." Bob sang as he headed toward his office.

Dr. Hull sat for another moment, and then sighed again, "Retirement is starting to sound pretty good. Although I think Bob needs it more than I do." He pushed himself to his feet and sighing again, muttered to himself, "I think this is where I'm supposed to say, 'not on my watch,' but then maybe I'm too uptight about this dignity thing. Maybe I should loosen up more. What was it they said at the last seminar I attended? Ask yourself if it will matter in twenty years and if the answer is 'no' then forget it.

As the tune wound its way through his head, a small smile crossed his face. "Bob bob bob bob barber an," he started to sing under his breath as he headed back down the hall to his office.

Chapter 18

Drew pulled into the driveway. She felt exhausted. She felt exhausted physically, because she had taken Dr. Evans's advice and kicked the daylights out of the ball. She felt emotionally exhausted because of the situation with Karen. *How can I face her again? Class is less than twenty-four hours away. What am I going to do?*

"I wonder if a woman can join the Foreign Legion," she asked Cocoa the cat through the car window, as he came to greet her. She opened the car door.

"Don't you dare jump on my car! I just washed off your previous cat prints. You can come sit on my lap for a minute." Cocoa seemed to understand that she needed a cat to cuddle. He leaped on her lap and rubbed his chin against her cheek. She put her arms around the big cat and held him close, burying her face in his fawn colored fur. Cocoa usually didn't like to be held, but he seemed to be making an exception for Drew.

Drew sat with her head down. She didn't hear Papa come out of the house, but out of the corner of her eye, she noticed some movement. Raising her head, she saw Papa making a silly face at her through the windshield. She smiled at him in spite of her bad mood.

He walked around to the open driver's door and peered in at Cocoa and Drew. "Will wonders never cease? Drew, How did you ever get Cocoa to sit on your lap? I've been trying for years. Maybe today's trauma mellowed him."

"Trauma?"

"You know how he likes to crawl into car and truck windows?" he asked.

She nodded.

"I washed my Buick today and vacuumed it out, then I remembered that I needed to go to the hardware store, so I hurriedly closed all the doors and the trunk, jumped into the car and started to back out of the driveway. I heard this bloodcurdling scream. I thought I'd killed Cocoa. I stopped the car and jumped out thinking I'd run him over. No cat under the tires. I looked under the hood, no cat, thank God. I got back in the car and started to back up again. Another scream split the air. Cocoa had crawled into the trunk to sleep. He was one upset feline when I finally opened the trunk. He flew out like his tail was on fire.

Cocoa looked up at Papa with his deep blue Siamese eyes. He meowed loudly and stared at Papa. His whiskers twitched, and he seemed to be saying to Papa, *Don't you ever do that to me again.*

Papa started using his singsong voice, "There's my handsome guy." He reached for the cat. Cocoa hooked his claws into Drew's stomach so that Papa couldn't grab him.

"Ouch, that hurts, Cocoa," she said as she pried his claws loose.

"I don't think he trusts you anymore," Drew grinned. "Here, Cocoa kitty, let's get out of the car, sweet baby." The cat still wouldn't budge when she tried to get out of the car.

"Turn the engine back on and he'll be out of there." Papa said.

"As long as I don't get clawed to death in the process." She reached for the key and Cocoa took the hint. As he was getting ready to jump down he threw a look over his shoulder that seemed to say, "That's right, pick on the cat, see if I sit on *your* lap again."

"Oh, Cocoa, I'm sorry." Her words echoed in her ears. She looked up at Papa. "I've been saying I'm sorry all day. Oh Papa, I was so bad today." Papa walked around the car, opened the passenger seat door and slid into the seat. Drew told him about her horrible day. When she finished Papa said, "You're sure a chip off the old block. If you only knew how many times your grandmother's mouth has gotten her into trouble. This would be nothing. But I have learned that time does heal and it will be okay. Things have a way of working out. Pray about it. Something good will come from this. Listen to Papa. Papa knows best," Papa said as he wiggled his eyebrows and smiled his shy lopsided smile.

"Oh, Papa, I hope so."

Chapter 19

That night, Drew reluctantly got down on her knees beside her bed. "Dear God, I really don't know what I'm doing, but I know I need help with this Karen situation. Please tell me what to do to fix it. Thanks. This is Drew, in case you forgot my name."

Bob had started to come into the room, and then he noticed Drew on her knees and heard her soft whisper. It tugged at his heart to hear her pray like that.

"Oh, Honey," he knelt beside her and put his arm around her, "God doesn't forget names. Before the beginning of time God knew you, before you were formed in your mother's womb, He called you by name; He's not going to forget you."

"Now you sound like Gran," she muttered.

"The Bible's got some good stuff in it."

"How would you know? When do you read the Bible?"

"I have one in my desk at work," Bob said.

"How come you never said anything before?"

"And get attacked? I just *look* stupid," Bob said sheepishly.

Drew laughed, "If I had to describe how you looked, *stupid* would be the last word I'd use." She looked up at his face reflected in the light from the streetlight outside, "Handsome, athletic," she sniffed his neck, "charming, sexy, irresistible, heavenly..."

Chapter 20

In the morning Drew helped at the clinic, anything to keep her mind busy. She wore blue jeans, a T-shirt under a light jacket and tennis shoes. Gran didn't care what she wore as long as no skin showed at her waistline. She arrived around 10 AM. Classes were already in progress. Aromas of cooking wafted from the kitchen, aroma therapy candles burned and the breeze blew through the open window carrying the fragrance of Sweet Peas combined to make a welcoming atmosphere.

Most people came for two weeks; they had dormitory rooms at the back, and there were classrooms, one large lounge area and a dining room. Gran had expanded on her first concept. She still kept the dining room and classrooms to educate people on healthy eating habits, but had discovered that alienation, either from society at large or from the immediate family, was a large factor. Many people ate for comfort or as an answer for loneliness. The lounge area, besides having the usual seating for conversation, had art supplies, musical instruments and tables for games. The idea was to provide healthy distractions from food. It seemed to be working.

Drew took off her jacket and hung it on the hook in the small room beside the restrooms. She shot back around the corner to see Gladys, a volunteer, crawling around the floor on her hands and knees.

"Hey, good for you, Gladys. I've heard crawling is great for brain development, prevents dyslexia and is a great way to keep slim. I'm so impressed," Drew said.

Gladys rolled to one hip and grinned up at Drew. Gladys was in her late thirties, had bright red hair, freckles, and a contagious smile.

"Then, I'll have to do this more often. Actually, I dropped my earring when I took it off to answer the phone. It tried to run away, but it couldn't hide from the long arm of Gladys Ruskin." She held up the errant earring in triumph. "Will you take over for me so I can take the Yoga stretch class? The lady that teaches it is really good."

"Sure," Drew said as she reached out and helped pull Gladys to her feet "You'd better hurry. You don't want to set a bad example by being late." Gladys gave her a thumbs up sign as she disappeared through the changing room door.

The phone rang constantly for the next two hours. Between doctors seeking information, possible patients, news media and curious people, Drew understood what Gran had been talking about. No more talk shows for a long time. Even so, they were going to have to expand again.

Essentially Gran and company had three separate functions going on. Initially, the clinic was a resource for people in physical danger– people suffering from obesity and other chronic conditions, with high C-Reactive Protein scores, (measures inflammation), or in emotional crisis. These desperate people had tried everything and failed. They checked in for two weeks. When they first arrived, they were assigned a room, given time to get settled, and then told to report to the main classroom for orientation.

The program was three-pronged: care for the physical body, the emotional health, and the spiritual. They went to classes to learn about food and food preparation. They learned what foods to avoid, and where to buy organic produce. They were taught organic gardening techniques for vegetable and herb gardens.

Their meals were served in the dining room with white linen tablecloths, silver, and candles. They had a choice of three different meals. The menu followed the guidelines of a high fiber, low carbohydrate combination diet (low carbohydrates, organic high fiber fruits and vegetables, and free-range beef and poultry, and 'wild caught' fish).

The 'New Adventurers', as Gran had labeled them, checked in on Sunday evening and stayed for two weeks. After prayer service, the "A" team members were sent for evaluation to a team of diagnosticians, which included doctors, nurses, chiropractors, an acupuncturist, and an iridologist who identified problems in the body by studying the iris.

Next were interviews and blood work, supervised by two on-staff doctors. Their first 'health class' followed, and subsequent discussions usually lasted until ten. Most were not happy to be fed a tablespoon of shark or cod liver oil but they had been primed for it so they cooperated, and many were surprised to find out there was only a slight lemon taste.

Their "green fast" started in the morning. They had a green drink for two meals and either a huge green salad (no iceberg lettuce), or green vegetable soup for dinner. The following days, they got real food, all range free organically fed meat, goat, chicken, wild Salmon or other fish. Snacks consisted of raw almonds, carrot sticks and berries. Later, other fruits and vegetables were added. If *adventurers* had colon issues, the greens were ground in a blender, and they drank their veggies. Much to Drew's disappointment, white potatoes were never part of the menu.

Bicycle and walking trails crisscrossed the green lawns. The owners of the adjoining property had horses, which they rented out to riders and offered classes for novices. Participants were encouraged to get into an exercise routine they enjoyed.

The second aspect of the program dealt with really sick people. Most were stage four cancer patients, but some had kidney, liver or other organ problems. There were people who had been sent home to die, and were willing to try anything.

Their systems were flushed of toxins and then pumped full of antioxidants and the immune boosters, vitamin C (3000 mg),Echinacea (herb) and Transfer Factor, every 4 waking hours. Drew had been amazed how much improvement was made, even in two weeks. Of course the people had to stay on the program six months, but they could come in as outpatients or continue with their own doctor in their home area.

The clinic had only been operating for a year and a half. Word was starting to get out. Each day more and more calls came in, seeking information. After each TV show, they got swamped with calls. So far, they treated or were treating a total of 125 patients. They lost three patients. In two of these cases, the patients began to feel so good that they got cocky and went off the program. Gran speculated that either they didn't like the discipline and hard work involved, or else so much damage had been done to their systems that their bodies couldn't recover. The third case caused Gran many tears.

A friend of hers was convinced that there was no cure for his type of lung cancer. The doctor had told him he only had three months to live but insisted that he be pumped full of chemo therapy drugs, even though the doctor said it would do no good. Her friend lost his hair, his memory, he didn't recognize his fellow wood carvers and he could no longer carve or drive.

Gran and his wife had brought him back from the first chemo encounter and a year later, he was doing really well; he could drive himself to the carving club, his hair grew back, he laughed and joked and started carving again. The lung tumor was shrinking. Gran thought they were coming down the home stretch, until the doctor insisted on giving him a 'killer' (the doctor's word) dose of a new chemo drug.

Gran and his family had to watch in horror as he deliberately started to shut down. He refused the immune booster, Transfer Factor, vitamins, reflexology treatments and rebounder, (mini-trampoline) therapy because it made him *feel better.*

"The doctor said I'm going to die right after Christmas," he said.

True to his doctor's word, he died right after Christmas, and at his funeral, his wife told Gran that she had found two unopened bottles of Transfer Factor in his personal effects.

A lady called in to see if tours were allowed. She and four friends lived in the area and wanted to know more about the clinic. Drew told her to come at 1:45 PM, and she would give the ladies the grand tour. Gladys would be back by then.

At precisely 1:45 PM, four attractive, older, well-dressed ladies bustled through the front doors and made their way over to Drew.

"Hi, you must be Drew. I'm Nadine Buckholder," she said as she reached out to shake Drew's hand and introduce her friends. Drew liked them immediately. She had them sign in.

"Since the dining room's is right here, we will start with that," Drew continued, "Basically, what we discovered is that people have poisoned themselves, either from the food they eat, the water they drink or the air they breathe in their own homes. The use of pesticides and non-organic fertilizer on food crops not only poisons our food but also decreases the nutrition value up to eighty percent.

"Some people don't know that chlorine in the water supply is a deadly poison and that it is absorbed through your skin. Your liver and kidneys need to work overtime just to detoxify your body. The air inside your house is extremely toxic also. The plastics in new carpeting, paints, cleaning chemicals, treated fabrics, etc, emits toxic fumes. When you come here, we try to remove most of the toxins that you have been exposed to. We teach you how to do liver, gallbladder, and kidney cleanses. Our water is filtered: the food is organic, and we grow a lot of our own fruits and vegetables. For example, raspberries are in season. You can walk out in the morning and eat the berries right off the bush. They taste incredible." Drew almost salivated at the thought.

They headed toward the classrooms.

"The first classroom," Drew explained, "is the 'food' room'. People are taught about food additives and why they should use only foods grown without chemical fertilizers, toxic herbicides and pesticides, and avoid GMO's (genetically modified foods), as well as avoiding all processed foods."

"All of them? What about some of the new things out like the margarine that lowers cholesterol?"

Oh boy, Drew thought. *Here we go.* "Cholesterol is necessary for proper brain function. In fact, there are some studies that show it if we reduce our cholesterol below 250 that our memory may become impaired. Your liver makes cholesterol, which is why we believe that drugs used to lower cholesterol, damage the liver. Cholesterol is not a good measure of health. If the product has hydrogenated oils or partially hydrogenated oil, they are just a mass of chemicals that your body doesn't know what to do with. The chemicals are poison to your body and do an incredible amount of damage. Chemicals destroy the balance that is needed to keep your body functioning properly. For example, did you know that there are bacteria that grow between our teeth, and works their way through our gums and into our bloodstreams?"

"No," Nadine said "not in my mouth. I floss and gargle twice a day."

"She does the same in her home. She's right. No self respecting bacteria would dare show their face in Nadine's house," laughed one of her friends.

Drew hesitated, sighed, and then said, "There can be such a thing as too clean a house. We need good bacteria to keep the bad bacteria in line, to speed healing, boost our immune system and help our digestive tract. If you use a lot of antibacterial cleaning materials, you destroy the balance.

"Now back to the bad bacteria between our teeth . . . Did you know that you can add seven years to your lifespan by daily flossing?" Drew said.

"No," the ladies said in unison.

"You are kidding, right?" Nadine said.

Drew shook her head. "Has your dentist ever given you antibiotics to take before you go in to have dental work done?"

They nodded.

"Why?" Drew asked.

"So we heal faster?" Nadine ventured.

"No," Nadine's friend, Sybil said excitedly. "I feel like a kid in school. I know the answer, pick me! They want to kill that bacteria between our teeth that you talked about."

Drew gave her the two thumbs up sign, "Any guesses about what happens when they get inside the blood vessel?"

They were quiet. Finally Nadine grinned and said, "They hitchhike to the heart."

"Well, sort of. They attach to the blood vessel walls and cause inflammation by making tiny tears in the vessel wall." Drew looked from face to face. "Now for your last semi-technical question. Are you ready?"

Sybil looked like one of the students on *Smarter than a Fifth Grader.* "I'm ready!" she said.

"Your body's maintenance guys come along, find the damage in the vessel wall and patches it with, guess what?" Drew asked.

Sybil looked stunned, like she'd run into a brick wall. "Come on brain, give me an answer. Wait a minute, what have we been talking about? Cholesterol. Our bodies use cholesterol like a bandage." Sybil said.

"You've got it," Drew said with a grin.

"Are you saying that the drug I'm paying a lot of money for is not saving me from having a heart attack, but is actually harming me?" Nadine asked.

"I can't say anything about your medication, but let me ask you question, do you have to go in periodically to have your liver checked?" Drew asked.

"Yes, I do. OK," she took a deep calming breath, "OK, say I can't get over the concept that cholesterol has to be low, what can I do to bring it down?"

"Get off partially hydrogenated fats, get water filters for your drinking water and your shower head, take a heaping teaspoon of whole golden flaxseed or other fiber, every morning, and take shark or cod liver oil for your dose of omega threes. One of the best cholesterol reducers is grapefruit, but you must **not** combine grapefruit juice with statins."

The women were frantically trying to get notepads out of their purses to write the information down.

"Don't bother to write it down because I have a handout. Basically, read labels, avoid chlorinated water, you can buy filters at the hardware store and the flaxseed at the health food store. I eat mine on my organic grapefruit every morning. It takes one to three months to get your body normalized."

"Okay, I understand the flaxseed and the avoidance of hydrogenated, non-organic foods, but isn't chlorine good? Doesn't it save millions of lives?" Nadine asked.

"Chlorine is a deadly poison. It kills bacteria very effectively, so what do you suppose it's doing in your body? It kills the good bacteria all through your digestive system, which are necessary for health. All your organs have to work overtime to neutralize the chorine before it kills you."

Sybil asked, "Why the shower filter? Don't we want the chlorine to kill germs?"

"We used to think that our skin was impervious, now we know that many things are absorbed right through the skin. Chlorine is one of those things. It gets into your bloodstream almost immediately.

"Here's the exercise room," Drew said, grateful to be able to stop lecturing. She was getting sick of talking about the same things over and over. In the future, she would just say, "Here's the lecture room, here's the exercise room, etc, or even better, here's the hand out."

As she opened the door, music and laughter erupted from the room. Gran was teaching a rebounder class. They had mini-trampolines set up in a big circle around the outside edges of the room. The students were jumping from one tramp to another in time to Christian rock music. They seemed to be really enjoying themselves.

"Oh, this looks like fun. Are outsiders allowed to come?"

"No, I'm afraid not. We don't have the room, but we do have former students who have opened a small health club of sorts, and they run classes very similar to ours. I'll give you their phone number."

Wonderful smells drifted from the kitchen.

"Oh that smells heavenly. I thought healthy meals would taste and smell awful. Can we stay for lunch?" Beth asked. The others nodded in agreement.

"You certainly can. We have limited facilities for the public but we can handle about fifteen extra people. We work on a first come first serve basis. Many former members wanted a place to regroup so we added three tables. The money we make from the restaurant helps subsidize those who don't have the resources to pay. We've just added three more tables to keep up with the demand."

After the ladies left Drew worked at the reception desk with Charlotte who had replaced Gladys.

Gran had a towel around her neck as she exited the exercise room and came out into the reception area.

"Drew, what are you still doing here? You'll be late for class." She looked at Drew closely, "Are you trying to pull a Papa? You're trying to avoid Karen, aren't you? Drew Richardson, I've never known you to be a coward; now go!"

Drew wrinkled her nose and said, "Rats." Without saying another word, she turned, grabbed her jacket and purse and left for class.

She felt like a condemned person as she trudged up the steps to class. "I don't want to face Karen", she said aloud in the stairwell. Somehow she felt better hearing her own voice echo in the deserted stairwell. "I don't want to face Karen, I don't want to ... but I have to. Rats, rats and double rats. Why couldn't I have kept my mouth closed? But nooo, mouth of the month had to flap. How can I face her? Rats," she mumbled as she reached the top of the stairs, opened the door, then let it close. "Now it begins," she said with a sigh.

The door to the classroom was open, so she took a deep cleansing breath, overcame the desire run back down the hall, and crept to her seat. She didn't look at Karen but kept her eyes on her notebook.

"Okay, class, let's go," Dr. Evans directed.

Drew looked over at Kevin. "What's going on?"

"We're heading to the lab. We're going to take a computer test and then run the results statistically so we can have a hands-on demonstration of what we've been studying," Kevin informed her.

Karen came up to her. "Can I work with you?"

"What?" Drew looked dumbfounded. "Oh, err, yeah, sure."

Karen put her hand on Drew's arm. "I'm so sorry about the way I acted. I know you really didn't mean to hurt me."

Drew stared at Karen, "Are you kidding? I said terrible things to you."

"Yes, you did, but in a way, you did us a favor. If you hadn't reduced me to a pool of tears, Bob and I wouldn't have spent the whole evening discussing everything. He said that he had been reading some articles from people at work; it seems everybody wants to help, and several of them are in line with what you've been saying. He wants you to give me the details of the vitamin E therapy. I know you wrote it down for me before, but I threw it out." She saw the look on Drew's face, "I know, I was wrong, but I didn't want to believe I had something to do with my baby's death. Bob said he'd been thinking about it and decided if we didn't try this, we'd always wonder if we could have had our own child. I remember you said there were two vitamin E's, one man-made and one natural and that the man-made was worthless. If my blood pressure is normal, I should use 1000 units. You said Bob and I need to take it for three months before we try to conceive. I don't remember which vitamin E was which."

"Wow, you did listen." Drew took a piece of paper out of her notebook and sat down at the workstations. She wrote D–ALPHA Tocopheryl or D' mixed tocopheryls.

"This is the real vitamin E. If the bottle says <u>Dl</u>-alpha tocopheryl, or Dl mixed tocopheryls, it is synthetic. The synthetic adds an 'l' after the 'D'. If it has an 'l', it's made in a lab.

"Both of you should start taking 1000 units of vitamin E three months before you plan to conceive. Oh, that's right, you know that. Switch to filtered water, dump the diet drinks, it's OK to have occasional chocolate, (preferably dark)(watch out for hydrogenated or partially hydrogenated oils).

Occasionally you can have something that's really bad for you, but always make sure that you eat a good balanced meal before you indulge. They offer health classes at the clinic. The fee is very inexpensive. It's probably the best investment you can ever make. If you can't do that, the library has a bunch of books on prenatal nutrition."

"Excuse me, guys, but I'm trying to teach a class here," Dr. Evans said.

"Oops, sorry," Drew said.

Chapter 21

When Drew got back, Gran was outside building a Windsor block wall in her raspberry garden. She had the truck backed into the side yard and was hauling the blocks to the tailgate where she could unload them. Gran had already completed the first layer of two rows and had nearly completed the last row. She had smudges of dirt on her face and a spot on her nose.

"You'll never guess what happened," Drew began.

Gran looked at Drew's happy face. "Well, Karen must have come over to your side of the issue."

"How did you know about Karen? Wait a minute, you mentioned Karen at the clinic. Papa squealed, didn't he?" Drew said.

"Well, he did, but only because it was necessary." Seeing the frown that crossed Drew's face, she continued, "He was concerned about you, so he told me what happened and we discussed it and prayed about it. I take it, prayer worked."

Drew looked uncomfortable. "It must have," she admitted, " I can't see how such a turn around could have happened on its own. It was very interesting; I'll have to think about it."

"Well, I'm thinking about throwing in the towel, or should I say trowel. My back is beyond quiet protests and is now in total revolt."

"Do you want me to massage your shoulders?" Drew asked.

"Is the Pope Catholic? Yes, please."

Later that night, Drew walked into the den looking for Bob.

"Aha, I found you. What are you doing?"

"If I were a betting man, and I am, in moderation, I would say that I'm watching the Olympic trials for ice skating. And if you were a thinking woman, you would know who I'm watching."

Drew's mouth fell open as she remembered. "My own cousin is in the Olympic trials and I forgot. Oh, my gosh, I forgot. Lexi will kill me if she finds out I almost missed her! How's she doing? Has she been on?"

"I think she's on next."

Drew looked intently at the screen. Her cousin was indeed the next woman on the ice. The announcer said her name, and she skated to the middle of the rink and paused as she waited for her music. According to Lexi's mom, Carrie, Lexi was not a passionate skater, but she was a dogged one. She had determination, she tried her best, proving her great grandfather's maxim, "I just ask that you try, and if you try hard enough you can accomplish anything."

"Wow, she *is* good," Bob said.

All of a sudden Drew burst out laughing. Bob glanced over at her. "Hold that thought until she finishes."

Lexi skated flawlessly.

"Wow, way to go, cuz." Drew whispered. That was the best performance Lexi had ever given.

"OK, tell me about the laugh."

"When you mentioned 'good' it reminded me of Lexi telling me about the time she tried out for band in Junior High. Up until then she was successful at everything she did. When she tried out for band it was a disaster. She had no idea what kind of instrument she wanted to play, so she just showed up in the band room. All the kids were trying out different instruments, and most were having trouble with the wind instruments. Lexi couldn't blow hard enough for the clarinet, so the band teacher had her try the tuba. Lexi tried to blow into the tuba but wasn't having much success. The band teacher told her to hold it up higher on her shoulder. The tuba was so heavy that both Lexi and the tuba went over backwards. Lexi was ok, but the tuba didn't fare so well. Then the bandleader handed her a trombone, and she hit him in the head with the slider thing. She ended up with the trumpet because it was light, she could blow it, and it had no moving parts that could leap out and hit people."

Bob smiled at the picture of Lexi holding a tuba and laying flat on her back with her feet in the air. It was hard to reconcile that picture with the graceful young woman that had just floated across the screen.

Drew realized she was holding her breath as they waited for Lexi's scores to be announced.

"Oh, my God," she screamed, jumping up and down, "Bob, she made it! She's going to the Olympics!"

Chapter 22

Gran had an appointment with Greg at ten AM at the police station. She was hoping that Greg would have some really good news. She had a difficult time thinking about the incidents as murder attempts because they had seemed so harmless. Well, OK, maybe not harmless, but so inept, they seemed harmless in her eyes. She had rather enjoyed the exhilaration of running up that steep hill and leaving the two assailants in the dust.

She parked and took the steps two at a time. *I would sure like to get this whole thing taken care of. I don't want Drew involved again.* She glanced at the duty officer. "Hi Frank, how's your wife? Are you surviving?" She laughed.

He held up his bag of baby organic carrots. "They're not so bad when you get used to them. Lois is so much better. It's like I have a new wife. I can never thank you enough. Of course the guys here are a little upset about the lack of doughnuts. You'd better make a run for Greg's office before any of the on duty officers spot you." He laughed at the expression on her pleasant face. "I'm kidding. Lois has been making zucchini and pumpkin bread and sending it in with me. The guys love it. Stop by the break room and try some. And," he held up his stainless steel water bottle. "We donated a water cooler for the break room, so now we're not only becoming healthier, we're helping the planet. I'm even thinking about ordering some stainless steel water bottles with a cool logo on them."

"Wow, way to go. So that means you don't hate me for having a hand in getting rid of your donuts?" she teased.

"Lady, I think I love you. You gave me my little girl back. I was so worried about her, and now she's singing around the house. She has her energy back. We're taking dancing classes. She's the prettiest girl there, and the best dancer."

Gran had to smile. Lois had been one of their first successes. Years ago in Hawaii on vacation Gran had prayed to be allowed to heal God's people. He told her she would be allowed to heal but he had taken his own sweet time. However he **had** answered her prayer.

"You're like the turtle, Lord. Slow but sure, I wasn't even forty yet. And now I'm ancient. At least I don't feel ancient."

Greg's door was open. So she peeked in "Are you ready for me?" She asked.

"I'm not sure. Come on in."

"What's wrong?"

"Do you want the good news or the bad news first?" he asked.

"Good news? Bad news? I assumed when you called, that we had them."

"I'm not quite sure what we've got. The prints on the jeep don't match the prints on the cigarettes and the stolen car. Also, the pictures of the men on Drew's phone don't match the pictures on your phone."

"What? How could they not?"

"They don't even come close."

Confusion flooded Gran's face. "So we have two sets of bad guys?"

"It would seem so. Do you want the good news now? I guess I should say possible good news?"

Gran looked at Greg with total confusion.

"We brought two brothers in for questioning," Greg said.

Gran felt her hopes deflate like air leaking out of a balloon.

"And?"

"This where you come in. Come with me. You can watch the questioning and identify them if you can. We're pretty sure they are the ones involved with Drew."

"Hallelujah."

Greg stood up and came around his desk. He was hoping he was right. He had to smile at her enthusiasm. She made a good cheerleader for the health contingents. He led the way to the observation room.

Inside Gran could see a scraggly -haired skinny man who looked to be in his mid-twenties. Gran didn't recognize him. He looked nothing like the two men that she had encountered. He was missing his two front teeth so that he lisped slightly when he talked. The officer asked him his name and his whereabouts on the night in question. When the young man mentioned his name, Gran looked up. *I know that name.* She peered at the man's face beneath his long hair and beard. His face was pretty well camouflaged. However, when the other brother was brought in, his face did look familiar.

"Wait a minute." She could feel her brain clicking into gear. "Ask him if he has a … an aunt named Lucy."

He left the room and called the officer out. When the officer went back into the room, he asked, "Do you have an aunt named Lucy?"

The man's eyes widened, "How do you know that?" He looked wildly around the room. "Is someone watching us? Somebody's in there, ain't they?" He jumped up and tried to peer into the two- way mirror.

"Sit back down, both of you." The officer had to walk around the table, grab the scraggly one by his shirtsleeve and drag him back to the table. "I told you to sit down, and I mean it. Now tell us what happened. You were the ones at the library, weren't you?"

The two men looked at each other, and then nodded. The scraggly one spoke, "We weren't really going to hurt that old lady. We might a kicked her or smacked her a little bit, but that's all. We was real mad at her. But we wouldn't have done nothin' real bad. She went and messed things up, really horrible like. Aunt Lucy was going to give us all her money on account she never married and had any kids. The doctor only gave her three months to live. Then she went to that stupid clinic and the doctor says the cancer is gone, and Lucy is jumping around like a teenager. She's datin' an' everything. She might even get married. I was planning on getting new teeth, and we had a truck all picked out. Now we got nothin'."

"Why don't you just get a job?" the interrogator asked.

"Job? I don't like workin'. I guess I could make my woman go to work and not tell welfare."

Gran rolled her eyes in a fair imitation of her granddaughter. *Too bad they can't put those two winners to sleep, like they do with rabid dogs.* She caught herself. "Whatever we do to the least of these . . . boy, Lord, you're tough."

She looked at Greg, and her face softened, "You did a great job of investigating and I really appreciate all your efforts. It's frustrating

157

because it doesn't look like there's much we can do. They never really did anything. However, I am going to call social services to try to make sure he doesn't get any more money from our tax dollars."

"Lots of luck." Gregg said.

"Do you have the name of his girlfriend? Maybe we can talk her into getting her tubes tied so he can't reproduce himself." *I'm sorry, Lord, I'm being terrible. Jesus, you died for them as much as for me. OK, Lord, they're yours. Just keep them away from my granddaughter.*

She was quiet for a few minutes, "So that leaves the two losers named Sam and Bud who are out there somewhere, assuming they haven't killed each other yet."

Chapter 23

"Drew, Papa and I are going to the lake," Gran said as she carried a bag of food to the truck. Drew had just parked in the front of the driveway and was pulling her backpack from the back seat.

"Just like that? Drew, you're being abandoned."

Gran laughed, "Hardly, you have your very capable husband and two mighty attack cats for protection. And, oh, I forgot to tell you, Greg caught the two idiots that threatened you."

"You forgot?" Drew flew around the car and stood in front of her grandmother. "How could you forget? Who were they? Why were they trying to scare me? Or were they really out for you, like we thought?"

"Whoa, let me catch my breath. Yes, they were really trying to threaten me."

"Gran, how could you? Do you realize how much sleep I've lost worrying about you?"

Gran started to laugh, and then looked at the hurt expression on Drew's face.

"Drew, not that I'm saying that you weren't concerned about me, you have a good heart and I know you were concerned, but losing sleep? You sleep like a rock, or a hibernating grizzly bear. OK, you're right. I'm a terrible grandmother. I should have told you, and I meant to, but so much has been going on. When we found out who it was, it felt like a huge rock being lifted. You were safe and I didn't have to worry that they might have really been after you."

"OK, who was it?" Drew demanded.

"Do you remember Lucy?"

"That cute elderly lady that was given three months to live? She was our first big success. I loved her; she had, has, such a great sense of humor."

"Yes. That's the one. Well, she has two scallywag nephews that were upset that we, God and our health team, healed her, because her money was supposed to go to them and they had it already spent." (Gran did not miss the frown that crossed Drew's face at the mention of God). "And when it was suggested that they get a job to buy new teeth and a truck, the oldest one said he didn't like to work but maybe he could send his girlfriend out to work if they didn't inform welfare."

"You're not serious? He really said that? What a scumbag. Some one should have drowned him at birth."

Chapter 24

The lake shimmered in the late afternoon sun; the breeze fanned the leaves while Papa was chest deep in the lake, trying to figure out why the warning buzzer on the pontoon boat motor kept screaming its head off.

Gran turned the key off. "This is hardly the relaxing day I had envisioned for us. First I discovered Louie, the rat snake, had taken up residence in the driver's console on the pontoon boat, and then our ride around the lake ended up being a tow back to shore, and now, although you did get it to start, we can't get the stupid alarm to shut up. What are we going to do? Carrie is coming in with our granddaughter, Lexi and some of her school friends in two weeks and we won't be here to make sure everything runs smoothly. They are looking forward to using the boat."

"I'm doing the best I can. Why don't you pray about it? You pray about everything else," he said testily.

"OK, Grumpy, let's give this a rest. It's too hard to work on the motor with all the wave action on the lake. I know you don't want to tow it home, but it will be much easier to work on. Let's pack it up and go to dinner."

"You're right. You go drive the boat and I'll take the truck over to the landing and we'll load it up."

They got the boat out of the water, up on the trailer, and ready for their trip back the next morning. They both tried to enjoy the dinner and not think about the boat and the upcoming deadline of Carrie's arrival, but Gran could see Papa's mind working on possible causes of the boat's malfunction.

The next morning as they were just about to pull out of the driveway, Papa asked, "What did you do with the boat key?"

"Did you look in the kitchen drawer? That's where I usually put it."

"It's not there," Papa said.

Gran got out of the truck and went back into the house. Papa checked the boat and the garage. An hour later, they gave up and drove home without the key.

"Penn, try to remember what you did with the key."

"Oh, what a novel idea. I never would have thought of that," Gran muttered.

OK, Lord. I give up. What did I do with the key? Where is it? Please tell me.

"It's in the truck."

This truck ? Our truck?

"It's in the truck."

"OK," Gran said.

"OK, what?" Papa asked.

"God says it's in the truck."

"Well, I already checked the truck and I didn't find it," Papa said.

When they reached home, they unloaded the truck and when Drew arrived, Gran was inside the truck, pulling out seats, Papa's tools and her emergency supplies.

"What's going on?" she asked.

"We can't find the boat key."

"Is there some reason you're looking in the truck, instead of the lake house or the boat?" Drew asked.

"Maybe I'm going crazy, but I'm sure God told me that it was in the truck. But I can't find it."

"Well, I guess he's wrong. No one can be right every time."

"Drew, we're talking about God. He is always right."

"If you say so," she said as she turned and walked into the open garage.

Gran heard the door to the kitchen open and close.

I'm going on faith, here. If you said it's in the truck, it's in the truck.

She went back to the task of dismantling the truck.

Chapter 25

Two days later, they were back at the lake. Papa had purchased a new starter cover, complete with two new keys. He opened the garage door and went to the wheelbarrow to get his tools. He opened his cloth drill case.

"Oops."

"What's the matter?" Gran asked.

"I found the key. I remember putting it here, now. I apologize for accusing you of misplacing it." He looked over at Gran. He expected her to be upset with him because he had made her feel guilty about losing the key, but although she looked upset, she did not seem to be upset with him.

"What's going on?" he asked.

"The key was not in the truck."

"Well, He did find it for us."

"But He said it was in the truck and it wasn't."

When they got back home, Drew asked how their trip was.

"It was great. We found the key and got the boat working," Papa said.

"Hey, that's great. Where was the key?"

Papa looked sheepish. "I put it in my drill case in the wheelbarrow."

"It wasn't in the truck," Gran said.

"What difference does it make? You found it," Drew and Papa said in unison.

Later Drew found Gran sitting on the couch with her Bible on her lap.

"This 'truck' thing is really bothering you, isn't it? Why are you making such a big deal out of it?"

"For thirty years, I've heard a voice, God's voice, I thought. It was always right, always true, and now, the same voice was wrong. Don't you see, everything I've believed to be true is in danger of being torn apart," she sighed. "You don't suppose that 'truck' might be another name for wheel barrow, do you? Like 'keep on trucking' or 'I won't truck with that kind of thinking'?" Gran asked.

"That's kind of stretching it, isn't it? Well, you know, there's only one way to find out. I'll go get your old college dictionary." Drew darted off into the den and came back quickly. She already had it open and was scanning the pages, "truant, truce, Trucial Oman, truck . . .oh, this is creepy. The third meaning for truck is wheelbarrow. A truck, as we think of it, is the sixth meaning."

Chapter 26

Gran was down in her workshop, carving a life size wolf. Wood chips were flying all over the place. Drew seldom ventured down to the basement because she didn't like the smell of sawdust and having to crawl around table and band saws and half finished carousel horses.

"Wow. To what do I owe the honor of your presence?" Gran asked when she looked up.

"Your wheelbarrow thing has got me really baffled."

"I'm fine, thank you for asking."

"What are you talking about?"

"Usually there is a little ritual between people that acknowledges their presence, like, 'Hi, how are you doing', 'or great wolf'," Gran said.

"Great wolf? Yeah, he is unique. Here, let me try again." With that, she backed out of the room and closed the door. Two seconds later, she opened the door and said, "Hi Gran, how are you today? By the way, that wolf is sensational."

"Well, thank you, Granddaughter. Are you well?"

"Why, yes, thank you for asking," Drew said.

"Now what were you going to say about the wheelbarrow? I'm not sure I can help."

"Why didn't he just say wheelbarrow?"

"I have a theory, but I'm sure 'Miss 140', or whatever your IQ is, will think it's lame."

"Wow, what brought that on?"

"I'm sorry; it's just that no one listens to me. I get treated like an eccentric that stands on the corner and babbles. I am a very intelligent woman and my ideas are worthy of consideration. First Papa brushes off my observation about the wiring on the boat, "Oh, the boat wiring is only twenty years old and has been left outdoors in the rain and heat, but wiring can never be too old and we don't need new wire." So what happens? The wiring burns up. Then *you* belittle my concerns. The only people who take me seriously are your husband Bob and drug companies."

Drew came over and put her arms around her grandmother. "I'm sorry, Gran, I really don't mean to belittle your concerns. And I have nothing but respect for you and your ideas. I just don't understand this God thing. Sometimes I think I can feel a presence, a loving presence, but it's gone before I can get an understanding of it.

"Now please tell me your theory about why God called the wheelbarrow a truck."

"I think God may be making me trust him, even when circumstances indicate that I shouldn't. No, 'making me' is not the right term. He is helping me grow in faith, by showing me that I *can* trust Him."

Chapter 27

Gran parked her Jeep behind the newspaper office. She had an appointment with the Journal's editor, Michael Asanti. Gran always looked forward to their meetings. She could e-mail her column, and sometimes she did, but Gran preferred the human contact of delivering it in person. Michael had printed her column long before it had become syndicated. Of course the only reason for the syndication was because Michael had bought her idea in the first place and printed it. No printed column, no syndication.

Bud watched her walk down the street and around the front of the building. Tall bushes grew along the side of the building and shorter ones ran along the front path.

"OK, Dumbo, here's the plan," Bud said.

"This I gotta hear," Sam said sarcastically. His ego had been pretty damaged by Bud's insults, and his wife had thrown out his cigarettes, limited his beer, and was making him walk the neighborhood with her and the other ladies. He hated it. To make things even worse, she'd started feeding him Gran's menus, and raw organic carrots had replaced his beloved chips. He hated that stupid old woman. It was because of her that he'd almost had a heart attack, and now she was responsible for him losing his chips.

"The plan is," Bud repeated, "I run her down when she comes though those bushes and out into the street. If she manages to stagger onto the lawn, you wait by those trees to head her off."

"I don't have a good feeling about this." Sam said.

"Just don't screw up again."

Sam got out of the car, walked down the street past the waist high bushes, and across the lawn to the trees. Bud waited in the street behind the wheel of a stolen Lincoln town car, with one foot on the brake and the other on the accelerator. As soon as she poked her nose through the hedge, well, as soon as she stepped out onto the street, he would gun it and knock her from here to doomsday. He pictured her caught like a deer in the headlights just before her body flew over the hedge and landed in a crumpled heap. He got so carried away that he almost ran a teenager down. His adrenal glands went into high gear when a teenager came bounding through the hedge opening and across the street. He tried to train himself to look for brown curly hair, tan shorts and a red T-shirt.

"Bingo, here she is." He mashed the accelerator and the big car lurched forward so powerfully that he was thrown back against the headrest. He was not used to a V8 engine and the car shot forward out of control. It jumped the curb and for a moment became airborne. It plowed through the bushes and came to a stop wedged between them. There was no sign of Gran. "Where'd she go?" he wondered. He tried to drive forward, but the car's wheels couldn't find purchase.

"Sam, get over here and help me push this car," he yelled.

He threw the door open, then put one of his hands on the dashboard and the other on the steering wheel, while he waited for Sam to get in position behind the car.

"OK, one, two, three, push," he said. They pushed but nothing happened.

"OK, I've got another idea," Bud said.

"Oh, I can't wait," muttered Sam.

Bud stood on one foot and wedged the other one against the gas pedal.

"Not a good idea," Sam said from the rear.

"Shut up and push when I say. OK, push!" With Sam's weight on the back bumper, and Bud's foot on the accelerator, the car's tires spun, and then caught. The car leaped forward, wrenching Bud's leg and causing a horrible snapping sound from his arm.

Sam yelled, "Hey, wait for me," as the car's momentum carried it out into the middle of the lawn, taking Bud with it. "We have to get out of here."

"You'll have to drive, I can't," Bud said as he dragged himself over the bench seat to the passenger side, and Sam jumped into the driver's seat. Sam looked over his shoulder just in time to see Gran safely inside the newspaper building. She and several other persons stood at the doorway watching them. At least one person had a phone to his ear. Boy was he going to enjoy giving Bud a bad time.

"Now why couldn't *you* drive, Smart Aleck?" Sam demanded in an imitation of Bud's previous tone. "Wow, that was a great plan. What other goofball plans do you have? How about we rent a plane and skydive out and land on her?"

Bud didn't answer. He sat leaning back against the passenger seat. His balding head was dripping with sweat as he leaned it against the headrest. He felt bruised all over. His leg hurt like a son of a gun. He thought his ankle might be sprained. His arm felt broken. He felt along the upper part of his arm, *Oh, rats, it is broken. Now what am I going to do? How can I tell Sam that he's going to have to take me to the emergency room?*

Chapter 28

The smell of freshly baked cookies and the sound of an old movie on TV meant Gran was on a cooking spree. Drew followed her nose to the kitchen. "Mmmm, you're making cookies. Yum," Drew said as she hurried into the kitchen. "Can I take some to class with me?" she said as she picked up the big cat who was doing figure eights around her ankles and ruffled his fur along the side of his face. He scowled at her and tried to leap out of her arms. "No you don't, you can put up with me for a few minutes."

"If I have to put up with her for a few minutes, Cocoa, so can you." Gran quipped as she pulled the cookies from the oven.

Drew lowered Cocoa to the floor, and then reached for a cookie cooling on the rack.

Gran stopped her hand with the spatula.

"Wash your hands first, please."

Drew washed and dried her hands then grabbed the hot chocolate chip cookie and popped it into her mouth. When she had finished, she shed her backpack, walked into the dining room, and laid it on the dining room table. She came back into the kitchen.

"About taking those cookies to class..."

"No," Gran said as she started to use the spatula to remove the hot cookies from the ceramic cookie sheet.

"Wait," Drew said in mock horror, "you're not going to use that contaminated spatula to pick up those cookies, are you?"

Gran frowned and went to the sink to clean the spatula.

"And put that backpack up in your room. Just because I cleared off the dining room table, doesn't mean that it available for more clutter."

"You're kidding about the cookies, aren't you?"

"No, I'm making them for my wood carving group. I'm going to make them healthy in spite of themselves. Do you know where those idiots went to lunch last Thursday?"

Drew was still eyeing the cookies, "what? Oh, some fast food place, I guess. Oh, I bet it's the place that Papa likes that sells those little hamburgers and hot dogs. You didn't embarrass yourself, did you? I'll bet you stood in the hallway as they were trying to escape, and yelled something like, 'You're not really going to eat there are you? Don't you know what that will do to your colon?'"

Drew looked at Gran's face as a slight blush made it's way upward.

"Oh, no, you didn't! No wonder you want to bring cookies.

"How many guys are in your wood carving group?" Drew said, mentally calculating how many cookies she would need for her class.

"I have thirty-five, give or take a few, *but* I'm not sharing! You're old enough to make your own."

"How about if you measure the dry ingredients into this bag," she said as she handed Gran a plastic storage bag, "and I'll add the other stuff. Are there any more semi-sweet chocolate chips?"

"No."

"How about the milk chocolate chips?"

"You're not getting my milk chocolate chips."

"Boy, you're sure a grump today." She reached around Gran and peered into the cupboard. "Hey, you've got a whole bag of milk chocolate chips and after all those lectures you gave me on sharing."

Gran gave her a dirty look. "You're too smart for your own good."

"I'll edit your column for you," Drew said.

Gran stopped, "Deal, but you have to wait till I'm done. And you'd better clean up so well that no one would ever guess you were here. My column is on the counter over there."

A commercial blasted from the TV set. "Oh, I love this song," Gran said as she flung her arms up into the air and started jumping and kicking to the music. "We did an aerobic dance routine to this," she said just before she burst into the chorus.

Drew shook her head, "And I think *I'm* strange. You are out of control, Grandmother."

Papa yelled down from the bonus room, "Hey, quit jumping down there. You'll loosen the flour joists."

Gran slowed for a minute then danced into the dining room.

"Do that jumping and caterwauling out in the garage where the floor will hold up under your weight."

Drew smiled and said quietly to herself, "Papa, you are a master tease." She knew how easily Papa could push Gran's buttons. The music ended. Gran went to the bottom of the stairs and yelled up, "You don't value your life much, do you?"

Gran looked back at Drew and asked, "You want to take health cookies to class?"

"Well, they already know I'm related to you, and maybe when they taste how good they are, they'll realize that food can not only build strong and healthy bodies but can also taste good."

Gran tried to suppress her smile. "Cookies can save the world? Wow, that's asking a lot from a cookie."

"Isn't that what you're trying to do with your carving group?" Drew asked.

Ignoring Gran's frown, she continued, "You can get thirty five guys in that little room? I've been in there, and you must have people carving out in the hall."

"Just about. I keep threatening to bring in a sledgehammer and knock out the wall. Most of the guys are very handy, and we could enlarge that room in a day if they'd let us; I'm amazed at the different backgrounds and talents my carvers have. But the county bureaucrats have to hire an expensive contractor and wait a year to enlarge the Senior Center. Maybe I should do a column on the waste of senior talent.

"I considered writing a novel about the seniors solving a mystery about missing body parts but then I got too busy. I did make an effort to write down their backgrounds. Besides being very talented wood carvers, there are engineers, pilots, computer whizzes, electricians, detectives, shop teachers, tool and dye makers, mechanics and, we even have an ex-spy. Boy, you name it, and somebody in the group has done it," Gran said.

"How do their wives feel when you wax braggadocio about their husbands?"

Gran smiled, "I think by now they realize that I'm not a threat. Ten years ago, one of the carvers was getting high liver numbers so I gave him a bottle of Transfer Factor and did some internet research to find things to help him, you know, liver cleanses, detoxifying, that kind of thing. His wife got jealous. When I saw her at lunch one day, she came up and looked me right in the eye and asked why I was being so nice to her husband."

"What did you say?"

"The truth, I just mentioned that we had already lost two carvers in three months and that I didn't want to lose any more. She believed me, realized my intentions were honorable, and relaxed after that. At our age, there are so many more women than men, and many women want to marry again. Unfortunately for them, all my guys are married. We always have women stop by the class and make comments like "This is the place to be because it has so many handsome men." As I said, when you get to be over retirement age, men start getting scarce. It's rather like throwing raw meat into a tank of sharks." Gran laughed at the expression on Drew's face. "I'm kidding. All the ladies are very nice. One time we were invited to a retirement center for lunch and we were to bring our carving projects. We had a very nice lunch in a private dining room. The chef came in to meet us and explain the meal programs. Then they took us on a tour of the facilities. They were obviously trying to drum up some more business. I must admit, the facilities were very nice. The main dining room was rather elegant, with white tablecloths and silverware. We had to pass through the dining room on our way to the demonstration area. I was in the middle of the group, joking with the guys when six or seven women came rushing up to me. I wasn't sure what was going on because they grabbed my arms and pulled me away from the group.

"How did you manage to be with all those handsome guys?"

"Just come to the senior center on Thursday morning and they'll teach you to carve."

"Oh, you wood carve?"

"Yes."

"Show us some of your work." They started giggling. I wasn't sure if they were giggling at me or giggling at the thought of being closer to the guys. I suspected the latter. I showed them my eight-inch baby African elephant and my hunt scene."

"Oh, you mean the horse and rider in the den on the coffee table? That is cool. Were they impressed?"

"Oh, yeah, but not as impressed as they were with my ability to hang out with all 'those good looking men.' I still like to tease the guys, but I don't go down to the senior living place any more. I felt I was being hunted down like a wolf chased by helicopters. I don't care how many times they said, 'You're amazing.'"

"Does Papa get jealous?"

"Heavens, no. He knows I need a creative outlet where I can just be me. I can joke and kid around, and I don't have to solve any problems or," she peered into her bag of milk chocolate chips, "share my chocolate chips. You've been sneaking my chocolate chips and somebody's been going hog wild with my Co-Q-10." She held up the small white bottle and shook it. She looked at Drew. "How many have you been taking?"

"Just two at a time, but they work so well, I've been taking them for practice, as well as the games. Between them and the vitamin E, I can run forever."

"Well, there's hardly any left and I have a game tonight too. I'm old and I really need them. Fur would be flying all over the place if I had reached for the bottle of Co-Q-10 and not found anything. When were you going to tell me that we were getting low? Three practices and a game a week uses up a lot of pills, and they take over a week to get here after I order them. Maybe I should have you be responsible for ordering the pills and making dinner occasionally. I know you don't like to cook but then, neither do I, and when you graduate, you and Bob will have to know how to make it on your own. I know Bob can cook healthy meals, but I think I've been neglectful in not having you do some of the basics."

Drew gave her a look of displeasure. "What is this? Pick on Drew week? I do my own laundry."

"Well, partially, you usually get a little help in the folding department because you often leave your clothes in the dryer."

Drew gave Gran her cross-eyed look. Drew felt like the Yellowstone bear poster where the bear was laying in the middle of the road. He had tire tracks across his body and the caption read, "Sheesh, all I wanted was a cookie."

Chapter 29

Later that afternoon during her soccer game, she heard Gran's annoying "Whoop, whoop, whoop" when she'd scored a goal. *Oh great, she's hounding and embarrassing me.* Gran and Papa had come to 'cheer her on to victory', as they put it. Right now it seemed more like stalking. She still was angry with Gran. *I am being petty,* she thought, Gran was right, which was probably why she was angry. She should know how to plan and fix meals. *Here I get mad at parents who feed their children fried foods and soda for meals, when I'd probably do the same thing to my kids, not the soda, but it's just too easy to keep them quiet with french fries and chicken fingers;.* And I love french fries! *Even though' I've read that white potatoes spike blood sugar faster than straight sugar.*

She intercepted the ball and dribbled toward her opponents' goal. She was still angry and she took her anger out on the ball and scored. She was so wrapped up in her thoughts that she never heard the cheers when she intercepted the ball again. Drew knew she could be intimidating and she was. She narrowed her eyes and glared at the young woman in her path.

"Be afraid, be very afraid," she said aloud.

The young woman playing fullback, who was supposed to defend the goal from Drew's attack, looked like she was going to burst into tears.

"Soccer isn't for wimps," Drew growled as she shouldered her way past the girl, knocking her to the ground in the process.

Gran's words, "If you can't win fair, then you don't deserve to win," ran through her head. She scored the goal then went back to help the girl up onto her feet.

"Are you all right? I'm sorry."

The girl looked her in the eye. "Yes, I am, no thanks to you. But I do appreciate your coming back. You're so much better than I am that there really was no need to knock me out of the way with your shoulder."

Drew sighed. "I know that. I was mad at someone else and I took it out on you. Actually I was mad at myself. I really am sorry that I hurt you. Can you forgive me?" Drew asked.

"I'm a Christian so I don't really have a choice,"

Oh, great, now I've got God mad at me.

Seeing Drew's look of chagrin, the young woman smiled, put out her hand and Drew took it.

The bus filled with laughing noisy girls, pulled into the University parking lot. The girls jumped down from the bus, laughing and reliving the high points of their game. They congratulated each other on their successes. Drew was patted and high fived as she stepped down from the bus. She was still in her uniform while the others had showered. They were used to Drew's idiosyncrasies and accepted her anyway. They hadn't really listened to Drew's explanation of the fact that chlorine from the water was absorbed into the human body though the skin and did some serious damage, especially to the good bacteria in the intestines. *No one wanted to think about bacteria and intestines. That was a given, although not even termites could exist and digest wood without the bacteria that inhabited termite intestines.*

According to television, all bacteria were bad and deserved to be wiped out. Life is a balance.

Drew always waited to take her shower until she got home. Gran had filters on all the showerheads. At first papa gave Gran a hard time about her water filters until he looked it up on the Internet. He researched and found the best filters and now the whole house was equipped with state of the art filters. *You'd think he'd learn,* Drew thought as she started toward her car. *And then there was the microwave.* She smiled as she thought of poor Papa and his microwave. He came home one day to find his microwave oven in the garbage can. He came rushing into the house with the oven clutched in his arms, "Look what I found in the garbage can. Why would anyone want to get rid of my microwave? Penn, did you have anything to do with this? How could you? Where do you come up with these crazy ideas?"

Gran had rolled her eyes (a trick she had learned from Drew), "Put that back into the garbage can. It changes the molecular structure of the food so that our bodies can not use it."

"No way." Papa wailed.

"Yes, way." Gran countered.

"I'm going to look it up on the Internet."

"Be my guest."

Papa had run up stairs and researched.

Gran was in the living room when he came back down.

"Well?" she asked.

Papa mumbled something.

"Excuse me?"

She was greeted with another unintelligible mumble.

"Speak up, I can't hear you."

"You were right. But I hate to throw away a perfectly good microwave."

"Do you realize that your microwave is over twenty five years old? It deserves a retirement for lasting so long." Papa looked sideways at her. He was not a happy camper.

"I feel like I'm losing an old friend."

"Yeah, they just don't make things like they used to." Gran had agreed.

Drew smiled as she thought of Papa's 'funeral procession' to the garbage can with the huge microwave oven.

Chapter 30

Their soccer team had won tonight and would be in the play offs. Drew was on a high. She almost skipped to her car. The inside of the car was so hot that she had to open all the windows and turn the air on high, even though the evening was cooling down. Never patient, she wanted immediate results . . . like the game today. It had been fast and furious, slam bang, past the goalie, yes! She had scored four goals and made three assists. She loved to run. She loved the sheer joy of moving. She just thought it and her body did it.

Pulling into the driveway at home, she saw there were no cars. Where was everybody? Oh, yeah, Gran had a soccer game tonight and Papa and Bob were playing Trivia at the local restaurant. The evening was so nice that she didn't want to go inside. She walked over to the bench at the side of the yard and started to sit down. The slight breeze cooled her skin and dried her uniform. She could smell Gran's roses that climbed the fence behind her. She walked over and sniffed the roses. The red roses had more fragrance than the white ones.

She moved back toward the bench. A small bird, a Carolina Wren, who was perched in the ornamental cherry tree above her head, started chirping at her. He didn't like her getting too close. Last year, Papa had built a storage shed under the new deck. He made sliding doors that moved along a metal track. Unfortunately, when the pair of Wrens had built their nest this year, they built it on the sliding door track of Papa's storage shed. Whenever Papa went into his storage shed, or people went out on the deck, the small birds would hop across the deck in protest which was pretty stupid, Drew thought, because Gran liked to sit out on the deck and her cat, Cheyenne, was always with her and Cheyenne liked to hunt.

Sadly, now only one bird remained, and he claimed his spot on the top of the small flowering cherry tree.

"Poor little bird, do you miss your mate?"

Do you get upset, God, when one of your creations die? Do you hold the little creature in

you hand and regret that he is singing no more?
Does a tear run down your face?

She sat back and looked up at the little
bird. He was so perfectly made. His colors
blended and his bright little eyes watched her
intently. Her attention wandered to other parts
of creation.

She sat until the stars came out. It was
amazing; it was still light on the horizon, even
after the sun had set. "Well, God, I'll say this for
you, you do nice work. The trees that reach up
to the sky and tower above me; there are so
many varieties, and the birds, the colors, shapes
and sizes, incredible; and that little chipmunk
running along the driveway, he's adorable. It's
like you set up a whole universe then put it on
automatic pilot; you put in a sprinkling system,
rain, an automatic lighting and heating system,
the sun, of course. But if Gran is right, you *stay*
involved with your creations. I have trouble
believing that, as you know, I'd like to believe
you take a personal interest; I really would. It
would be nice to know that I was loved by the
one who created me. Do you love me?"

Drew sat back on the bench and rested her head against the top rail. Her eyes closed. Drew felt a joyful peace settle over her. She heard a car door open and close and heard feet walking along the stone path towards her. She opened her eyes and saw Bob looking down at her. She smiled, "Hi, Sweetheart, did you win at Trivia?"

Chapter 31

Gran was off to her weekly wood carving club meeting. Between the bag of carving tools, the life-size wooden polar bear head, her purse and the plate of cookies, Gran had all she could do to get into the senior center building without dropping anything. Fortunately, the doors opened automatically as she called a greeting to the ladies in the office. She was supposed to sign in but decided against it; and went on into the center, past the sign-in podium, and turned down the hallway to the right. She could hear the happy rumble of male voices as she walked toward the small room that was allocated to the carvers.

"There she is," Bob said as he jumped up to get her a chair, "and you brought cookies." They helped her download the cookies and get settled. Carvers were packed in like sardines so that when all her paraphernalia was settled, she had to squeeze between people and chairs to see what projects others were working on. Every project was different, just as each man was different. Sometimes half of them took a special class together like carving gnarled bearded old men out of mangrove roots or, carving roughed out Santa Clauses at Christmas time.

"I brought in some more patterns," Willard called from his usual spot in the corner. His pleasant face creased with a wide smile. Willard was active with several carving groups and always participated in the exhibits held by the National Park Service. He was such a good salesman that he would always end up selling whatever he was working on, and often got orders for dozens more. Willard fished through his bag for the patterns he had brought and handed them to Gran. She had begun organizing the patterns that the carvers had created or collected, into plastic crates and file folders she had purchased. The project had grown over the years to four crates. When a carver wanted an idea for a new project, he would find one he liked, then take it to the receptionist who would cheerfully make a copy for him.

Gran looked through Willard's patterns and found three that she wanted. "I'm going to make copies of these three patterns. Does anyone else want copies?" Four hands went up.

"OK." She took the patterns and went out to the receptionist's desk.

"Hello again, Ladies; is your day going well?"

"Yes, our day is going gloriously; we just finished the cook book. Would you like to buy one?

"Oh, I love old recipes," Gran said as she put the patterns into the receptionist's outstretched hand. She thumbed through the cookbook while she waited for the copies. There was a section on 'Healthy' recipes. Gran quickly turned to the page. There were two recipes; the first one was made with commercial pudding. "Now why would they think that was healthy," she muttered to herself, "don't they read labels?" The second one was made with a new artificial sweetener. "Oh, Lord," Gran said aloud, "not only is this not healthy, but it's downright dangerous. It causes kidney and liver damage. You could spend the rest of your life on kidney dialysis."

"But it's made from sugar,"

"Let me see, you're trying to avoid sugar, so you're making the argument that because it's made from sugar, it's healthy?"

"Well, I heard that it's safe. They even advertise how great it is. Haven't you seen the ad with the cute little girl in the swing? Besides, I'm sick of hearing how everything that tastes good is bad for me. You have to die of something."

Gran sighed. She opened her mouth to say, "At least keep it away from your children," but realized that the woman had reached lock down and to say anything else was useless. Frustration made her angry and she felt her insides start to simmer. She was angry at the greed of the manufacturers and angry at the people like this woman in the office, who preferred to stick their head in the sand. *You have to deal with things. You are expected to be responsible for your own health and for your children's health. God gave you intelligence and He intends for you to use it.* She remembered a man who stood outside the hospital yelling, "Why did You let this happen to me?" when he was diagnosed with lung cancer. He shook his fist at God while still holding a burning cigarette in the other hand.

"Lord, please protect the children." She prayed as she took her copies and walked slowly back to the carving room. "Well, that sure killed my good mood. Bummer."

Chapter 32

Gran and Drew headed out of the house together. They came through the garage so they could load Drew's bike in the back of Gran's Jeep. After they loaded Drew's bike, Gran said, "Oh I forgot that new CD for the aerobic dance class." She ran back into the kitchen and grabbed the CD off the counter. She ran back, opened the car door and started to fling herself onto the seat.

"Gran, no!" Drew exclaimed in horror as she shoved her grandmother back through the door.

"What in the world?" Gran said as Drew's momentum sent her sprawling onto the driveway. She rolled to a sitting position and looked up at Drew in amazement. Drew had talked back before, but she'd never knocked her to the ground. Drew's face was frozen in horror like a vignette in Madam Tousard's wax museum. Her eyes stared at something. Gran slowly rose to a standing position. Drew kept staring at something in the front seat. Her eyes followed Drew's. *What in the world?* She looked at the object wedged between the seat and the seat back. At first it didn't register, and then she realized that there was a large hypodermic needle sticking out into the seating area with the plunger wedged in the crease of the seat. The significance of it sent a cold shiver through her body.

Drew was already dialing 911 on her cell phone. Gran just stood there transfixed. "If I had been alone, if we had taken separate cars, like we usually do, I would have been stabbed by that thing. The force of my body weight would have injected me with whatever is inside the syringe. And whatever it is would now be raging through my poor little body." The more she thought about it, the more upset she became. "And then, when I was unconscious, or dead, they would have retrieved the hypodermic and everyone would have thought that I had a heart attack, 'some health lady she was'. Course I'm assuming there wasn't a deadly poison in it that could be traced. It obviously didn't contain something good like vitamin B12."

She started to shake in earnest. She had trouble walking. *Lord, your child needs a hug.* She stumbled several times while moving slowly back into the garage, through the kitchen, through the dining room and into the living room. She fell on her knees in front of her prayer chair. She visualized Jesus sitting in the chair, and in her mind, she crawled up on his lap and cuddled against his shoulder like a small wounded child. "Lord, I'm really afraid; somebody is serious about killing me. I know fear is not of you. Jesus, please just hold me tight. I know I'm shaking because I'm in shock. Heal me. Give me the peace that only you can give because you are the prince of peace." She felt him hold her close and his peace creep through every cell in her body.

"Gran, where are you? The police need to ask you some questions," Drew yelled.

Reluctantly, Gran took a deep breath and came back to the world of greed and hypodermics because it was also the world of beauty and loved ones. "Thank you for loving me," she whispered, as she got up and went back outside just as another police car was pulling up. The yard, the street in front of the house, and the street beside the house, were filled with fire trucks, ambulances, and at least twelve police cars that she could see.

"At this rate, we will know every one on the whole police force." Gran commented.

"Don't forget the sheriff's department. And I think there might be some FBI guys. The 911 guys kind of overreacted when they heard it was you. I called Greg too. He's coming with his crime crew. Are you OK?" Drew asked.

"I don't know what to say. I'm slightly overwhelmed to say the least. I'm pretty sure that I wouldn't be alive if it weren't for you." Gran put her arm around her. "Drew, you are incredible. You saw the danger and acted immediately. In answer to your question, I think I'm going to recover."

One of the police officers looked into the Jeep. "Holy cow! That needle is big enough to stop a hippo."

"Thanks a lot," Gran said. She frowned at the young officer. "Didn't your mother teach you never to refer to a lady's age or her weight? I resent the implication that a hippo and I bear a resemblance. What's your name?"

"Officer Terry Earhart. I'm sorry ma'am, I didn't mean to imply in any way that you were big." He blushed.

"Likely story," she teased.

The young man smiled, "Thank you, Ma'am."

Drew looked a Gran speculatively. "You seemed pretty upset when you disappeared and I see the remnants of tears. But now you're joking around. What's going on?"

"I just needed a little assurance. I'm OK now."

"You went into the house and prayed, didn't you?" Drew asked.

Gran just smiled, winked at her, and walked over to greet Greg as he pulled up in yet, another police car. His crew was right behind him.

"Boy, you're getting to be a celebrity; the mayor called my office and asked me to personally take over the investigation of this case. I didn't tell him I was related to you, and was already personally involved."

His team started taking pictures. The hypodermic needle was removed and placed into an evidence bag. Greg looked at it, "Man look at the size of this thing. This would take down a horse."

The look on Gran's face made him break out in laughter.

"I don't think you're a bit funny." Gran tried to keep a straight face when she said it but she didn't quite make it.

"You do realize that someone has probably just tried to kill you, and it's not those doofuses that made attempts on you in the past?" Greg asked.

"What attempts?" Drew asked.

"Yes, what attempts?" Papa's big voice boomed from behind them. *Oh no, what a time for the truth to come up behind me and bite me in the butt,* Gran thought. She hadn't noticed that Papa had returned from the dump. *Where had he found a place to park?*

Papa always asked so many questions that if she stayed to answer them she'd be late for her class. "I need to get out of here," Gran said.

"Forget it. You need to answer some questions," Greg said.

"Yes, Young Lady, you need to answer some questions," Papa said.

"Drew can answer questions far better than I can, and I'm sure she won't leave until she is sure that every possible clue is labeled, bagged, and pictures are taken from every single angle. She didn't watch CSI with Papa for nothing."

"Tell me about it. She's driving my crew crazy, but they've been keeping quiet because she's obviously very upset about the attempt on your life. Often she's had tears in her eyes. I can't remember when Drew's been so emotional." He looked at Drew speculatively and walked up close to her.

"You're not pregnant are you?"

"Greg, hush your mouth. Of course not. My dance card is way too full to make room for a little person. Depending on what I decide to do, I may have years of school ahead of me. Pregnancy would really kill the soccer deal. Why would you even say a thing like that?" She snapped at him. He held his hands up in front of himself as protection from Drew's look of death.

"No offense meant. Brandi got that way with both Cher and Michael, that's all. If you were pregnant, the whole family would be jumping up and down in excitement."

Drew rolled her eyes and walked away.

"Boy, that's all I need," she muttered.

"Drew," Gran said, "children are never convenient. But they bring such joy. Look how much fun Jeremy's son Andrew is."

"He is adorable, that's true, but would he be so adorable if I had to get up twenty times in the middle of the night and have to change diapers and hold him constantly when he's fussy while I'm trying to cook dinner?"

"You cook dinner? Boy, would I like to see that? I'd be glad to carry your baby around, if you'd cook dinner, or should I say, *finish* cooking dinner," Gran said.

"Boy, nothing like a death threat to get you all fired up."

Gran ignored Drew's comment. "When your Aunt Carrie was conceived, Papa and I were both in college and had only been married two weeks. Papa, very seriously, offered me $20 to have my period."

Drew burst out in laughter, "You're kidding? Right?"

Gran grinned back, "Twenty dollars was a lot of money."

Drew shook her head.

"The point, I'm trying to make is that there is no perfect time to have a child but it all works out. We adored her, and all of our children. I remember one day in particular. I came home to our small one bedroom apartment and went into our bedroom. Papa's grandfather's wedding gift to us was a king size bed that filled the room. We barely had room to squeeze Carrie's bassinette between the bed and the wall. Papa was laying on the bed, leaning on one elbow, looking at Carrie in her bassinette. He reached over and touched her little hand. "She's so beautiful," he said. I sat down on the bed beside him and we just watched our little miracle." Gran shook her head to dismiss the past.

Finally most of the vehicles had left or were in the process of leaving and soon the streets were clear.

"Free at last," Gran said. "OK, Kiddo, get in the truck and I'll drop you off at school." Gran drove Drew to school and made it to the clinic just a few minutes late for her rebounding class. Her students had already pulled out the mini-trampolines and had them set up in a big circle. They were ready to bounce to health.

After a rebounding class Gran only stayed long enough to answer a few questions. "Although I believe the lungs are the pumps for the lymph system, the rebounder has been shown to move it as effectively. The lymph system is the garbage disposal system. Try to imagine your kitchen, if no one took out the garbage. The lymph system dumps into the circulation system, right about here. She pointed to her chest above her heart. Jumping on the rebounder also creates electromagnetic energy which stimulates every cell in the body and does it without harming your knees and ankles."

Drew was back and waited beyond the doorway until Gran had answered the last question. She stopped when she saw Drew in the doorway.

"Boy, you have a lot more patience than I do." Drew said.

Gran smiled, "Your body doesn't come with an instruction manual. How will they learn if they don't asked questions?"

"I thought you said the Bible was the instruction manual."

"Well, yes it is, absolutely. The Bible goes into great detail about what you should eat and how to live, but most people don't read it or if they do, they don't take it seriously. Some theologians say it's not relevant for today; they say it's been paraphrased and doesn't mean what it says, so that we shouldn't take it literally, or they use it to prove their own point of view.

"People live in their bodies, but aren't aware of what a marvelous creation God designed for their soul to get from conception to death."

"Too theological for me, Gran." Drew said as she ran ahead.

"I doubt it; come back here, you little rascal and I'll buy you lunch." Gran called after her.

They left the classroom area, walked to the far side of the dining room, and sat at a table next to a window. The window overlooked the lawn, and the landscaped gardens.

Wonderful scents came not only from the kitchen, but also from the flowers and herbs outside. The breeze carried the scent of spearmint, rosemary, and other herbs through the screened windows.

The waiter came and took their order.

"You know, if I ever do have kids, they are going to be super kids, just like your kids were."

"It's a lot easier now to keep kids healthy. When your mom was a baby, I worked my toes off trying to keep them healthy. A friend of mine gave me a book called *"The Poisons in your Food."* I remember walking down the grocery store aisles and looking at all the bright colored boxes. When I finally got the courage to lift a box down and read the label, I was shocked. There were six different unhealthy chemicals or preservatives in that box of cereal. How was I going to protect my children?

"Now, you can just walk to the health food section of almost any grocery store and buy healthy cereal or bread and organic produce. Then, you couldn't get organic food or whole grain breads, at least, not that we could afford, so I had to make everything from scratch. This wasn't as easy as it sounds. One time I set the house on fire when my homemade bread got stuck in the toaster. The bread burst into flames, and the flames burnt the wooden cupboard above it. For some reason, the firemen thought it was hilarious.

The kids got sprouts in their sandwiches and the other kids would tease them about *worms* in their lunches. Your mom said they used to wolf down their lunches so that they would be done before the kids started trading lunches. It may have been embarrassing for them, but they were the healthiest, smartest, and best looking kids in the school."

"You're not a bit prejudiced, are you?" Drew asked.

"The dentist raved about their teeth."

"Gran?"

"Me? Prejudiced? Absolutely not." she grinned at Drew. "They were all in some sort of gifted programs, and people were always coming up to me and telling me how beautiful my children were. Although, because your aunts, Carrie and Anne had short hair, I was often told how beautiful my *boys* were. They did not appreciate the compliment, so to this day, they wear their hair long.

"The point I'm trying to make is that besides being beautiful, smart and good natured, they were *never* sick. Of course, besides all the health food, I gave them enough supplements to kill a horse, and the effort was worth it."

"I remember the story about Aunt Carrie calling you from college and complaining about having had pink eye and being sick all the time and whining, 'What's the matter with me?' because she had never been sick before."

Gran half smiled. "That's true."

"I still think you're prejudiced."

"Drew, I love you, but sometimes you are a pain in the rear."

Drew laughed, a beautiful full contagious laugh, which caused all around her to smile.

"You know Gran, I just had a thought. I was thinking about Greg's comment and what if

I were pregnant. My first thought was no way; I still have the rest of this year, then maybe grad school. How can I do that? Then I thought, *other people do it.* You went back to school when you were pregnant. You even took Jared to classes with you and nursed him, discreetly, of course, in class."

"Drew, nursing in public, even discretely, isn't always so easy. The classes I was taking were early childhood education classes. What could they say? Nursing helps brain growth and reduces dyslexia." Gran saw the frustration in Drew's face. She was trying to put things into perspective. "Sorry, I didn't mean to interrupt."

Drew stared at Gran for a minute then her brain clicked back into speculation mode. "Well I was thinking that school and children might even be easier than having to work at a job all day, like most people have to. You said something earlier, what was it? It was something about your body having to get you through life to fulfill the plan God has for you? If God knows you before the beginning of time and calls you by name, before you were formed in your mother's womb, then what about the baby that's aborted? He gets conceived because he's meant to be conceived at a certain time. But what about the plan for his life? He gets the short stick. He never gets a chance to fulfill God's plan for him. He gets shot down before he even gets a chance to try. That's not fair." Tears filled her eyes.

Gran reached over and put her arm around Drew and kissed her cheek. "I take it there will be no abortion in your future?"

Drew was quiet a moment before she shook her head. "No, there will not be, but you know, it's so easy if you don't really think about it. If you just don't think about the fetus as a living breathing human being, as long as it's just *tissue*, like a cyst or a tumor, why not remove it?" she asked.

"When abortion came up in the Washington state ballot as a referendum, in the early 1970's, Papa and I became part of a group called Voice for the Unborn. They were such sweet loving people. I had a poster that said, S*terilization before murder.* They lovingly pried it out of my locked fingers and gently explained that convincing young women to find a loving home for their child was the answer. And I agree with that. Every child should be cherished.

"During that election, I was taking a yoga class at the YWCA, and in my class was a real women's libber. Both camps printed a newspaper. She asked me to read their newspaper. It was so full of false propaganda and misinformation that I looked at her in amazement, 'But none of this is true.'

"They wanted to win the election and they didn't care how they did it. They shamelessly ignored the truth and printed what they thought the voters wanted to hear so that they would take their side.

"Our newspaper had one numerical error, which we retracted because we wanted the voters to know the truth. I told her that I thought her newspaper was all propaganda and no facts. When I was handing out the Voice for the Unborn newspaper, in an old folks' home, they were there telling the people that they were old and had lived their life and as such, they shouldn't put their moral values on these poor young girls who found themselves pregnant and alone.

"The libber asked me what I thought about their newspaper. I said 'It's very poorly written and terribly inaccurate,' and I walked away to use the restroom. She chased me down the hall into the ladies' room. 'Women should have the right to choose, you can't deny them that right.'

"I came out of the stall and stared into her face. 'Women have rights. They can choose to have sex or not. They can choose to use protection or not, and they can find the baby a home or not. Where is their lack of choice? You know who's funding this election? Men, men doctors who will make lots of money, and boy friends who don't want the responsibility.' (At that time, all the people on the pro-choice election committee were prominent male doctors who stood to make a lot of money from that legislation.)

"She hated me after that, but I fail to see how women benefit from killing innocent children. Women have been given the right to kill another person just because they don't want him/her around. No other segment of our society has that right. Do you suppose that could be expanded to grown people? I'm a woman and there's a male child that I'd like to abort."

Gran was quiet.

Drew was quiet for a moment too, but then comprehension brightened her face. "You're thinking of Lucy's nephew and his scheme to get a new truck by making his girlfriend work two jobs and not tell welfare, aren't you? I thought you were supposed to forgive 'Ole Rat Face seventy times seven'."

Gran's jaw dropped. "Land of Goshen, Child when did you become a mind reader? I was just apologizing to God for thinking bad things about 'Old Rat Face.'"

"What terrible things were you thinking?"

"That he is the embodiment of the argument for abortion."

Drew laughed, "And here I thought that you were so holy."

"It's really not funny, Drew. It's really all about respect for life and whether we should decide who lives and who dies. At the same time the abortion issue raged, there was talk in the

Scandinavian legislature, of mandatory death at eighty," Gran said.

"Great grandma is 94 and still going strong. What's with that? What were they going do? Sneak up behind her and club her over the head?"

Gran had to laugh. "I think my mom would be okay. She can still walk them into the ground. If they tried to sneak up on her, the guy with the club would probably have a heart attack." Her words reminded her of her run in with Sam the smoker. The smile faded.

"Are you thinking of the attack on you at the church?"

Gran's eyes opened in surprise. "How did you know about that?"

"Well, for one thing, it was in the newspaper. And for another, Greg told us about it when he asked Bob and me to do some Internet research for him. We didn't tell Papa, but you need to talk to him soon before he reads it in the newspaper. He may already have seen it. If he did, he will be crushed that you didn't confide in him."

"It's the first time I've ever kept anything from him. I just couldn't handle the lecture, but you're right, he needs to know. He must not have read the paper or I would have heard about it. I'm not sure that I like having my life plastered all over the newspapers; in fact, I hate it."

"Gran, you have a syndicated column and you appear on TV and yet you're bothered about having your life 'plastered' all over the newspapers?"

"Well, normally, I choose what I want to have 'plastered', when I do the column and then I try to keep it centered on nutrition research and not on my personal life. Speaking of research, did you find anything?" Gran said.

"Bob found some interesting stuff and he's pretty sure it's the Hexal drug company. But how can we prove it? That in itself could 'prove' to be a real problem. Maybe if we can catch them in the act. I don't think they're using professional hit men, even though this was more sinister than the previous ones."

"My modern-day Nancy DREW–Bob can be one of the Hardy boys or... what's the new boys' sleuth team? The Carver cousins?"

"Gran, you are not taking this very seriously."

"Well, no one leaves the planet alive."

Drew cast her an, *I'm not believing this,* look.

"I'm really not worried about dying. I'll be with Jesus, and I'll see my Dad. I wish you could have met him. He would have adored you." Her face lost its wistful look. "Wait, I amend my previous statement. I'm not afraid of dying. At least I don't think I am, **but** I don't want any pain and no Alzheimer's. I want to go quick and painless. There, do you buy that?"

"I don't want you to talk about dying. When we find out who's behind all this, we're going to catch them, because between Bob and me, to quote Gladys, they can run, but they can't hide."

"I guess that means I'm in good hands."

"You bet you are. Hey, I just had a thought. The perpetrators must've been in the area so that they could retrieve the hypodermic."

"They wanted it to look like a natural shutdown," Gran said.

"I'll ask around the neighborhood to see if anyone saw anything,"

Drew said.

"You don't think Greg would've already done that."

"Oh, yes, of course he would. Greg would have figured the perp must've been watching and waiting to retrieve the needle. If you were out of commission, the perp would've retrieved the syringe and driven off. But, when he saw me push you out of the car, he must have known that his attempt had failed and he needed to make his escape. Then the police arrived and maybe blocked his escape route. No, he would have left inconspicuously before the police arrived. Oh, I wish I'd thought to take pictures."

"This is getting too complicated. I'm going to take a nap."

"A nap? Gran, you never take a nap."

"I guess murder attempts on your life wear you out."

Chapter 33

Greg felt he was well on the way to solving
Gran's case. Between Bob and Drew's research
in the newspaper articles, clues were pouring in.
It seems that someone *is* out to get Gran. Two of
the leads were from two employees of the Hexal
drug company. They did not want their names
mentioned if Greg questioned their boss, but
they said they would testify, if it came to that.
Greg was given the name of a doctor that also
worked for the firm. Greg planned to question
him himself. The folder in front of him on his
faux cherry wood desk was growing thicker by
the hour. Drew had practiced her faux cherry
wood technique on the ugly metal desk so that
at first glance, and second glance, the desk
looked like a real cherry wood. An imitation
Oriental rug graced his floor. It had been Bob
and Drew's birthday present to him. It was
against regulations, but nobody ever said
anything but cool or wow. He looked back at the
file. *I just about have you, you greedy son of a
gun.*

Greg walked out of his office, down the hall, into the main room and over to Detective Bentley's desk. He was impatient to be finished with this whole weird affair. "Have you heard anything more?" he asked.

"Unfortunately, we've gone about as for as we can. Hancock identified two women in the CEO's inner circle who admitted that they hired one of the women's relatives to 'nudge' Gran into the hereafter . . . "

"Don't you mean put her in the morgue?" Greg interrupted.

Officer Bentley continued as if Greg's outburst had never happened. "But Fitzsimmons, the CEO, never actually came right out and said, 'Kill the old lady.'"

"So we have nothing on Fitzsimmons? How frustrating. He's the one I want. The women probably will just get a slap on the hand. He's a slime ball and I want him."

"Dom and Rich went downtown to ask him a few questions. We did find some background information that might give us more insight."

Greg tried not to execute an eye roll. "I hate the word 'insight.' It just gives their lawyers more excuses to get them off. And I'll be willing to bet that Fitzsimmons has been bailed out more times in his life than Noah's Ark." Greg tended to see things in black and white. It was hard to care but, as Chief, he must also be fair. "OK, let's hear it."

"The senior Fitzsimmons started the drug company. Both sons went to college so they could take over when their dad retired. They were fiercely competitive so their old man decided to give them each a turn at being CEO. Sean (the one we're after) went first. He's pretty cutthroat and increased their sales by any means possible. He hired more marketing help, which was good, but then he pressured both the research team and the FDA to push drugs through before they were fully tested."

"So how does that differ from usual? Every day there are ads from law firms seeking people suffering dangerous side effects from taking drugs that have to be pulled off the market. Just today, I saw an ad from a law firm about Fostomax, a drug long prescribed for osteoporosis. My mom's been on it for years so that her bones would be strengthened; now they're saying that it can cause the thigh bones to become brittle," Greg complained.

"That doesn't make any sense. So you're saying that the drug that's supposed to help her, is actually making her condition worse?" Bentley asked.

"Apparently. Now my poor little mother is terrified about falling and breaking a hip. Do you think Fitzsimmons gives a rat's derriere about their customer's welfare?"

"Does Hexal Drug Company make Fostomax?" Greg asked.

"I have no idea. I would think that most drug companies make similar products. According to Gran, the idea of supplementing calcium is good, but they use the wrong form of calcium. They use limestone in various forms such as calcium citrate (limestone treated with citric acid), which doesn't build good bone. Calcium from plant sources or bone meal (from a safe source) are forms of calcium that your body can use. Oh, yeah, they should be combined with a walking program. Boy, do I sound like Gran or what?"

"As a matter of fact . . . now to get back to Slime Ball, I guess he's even more aggressive than the average CEO. He does whatever he pleases. He seems to think he's above the law because he's always been bailed out of trouble. He's never had to face the consequences of his actions.

"Are we going to change that scenario? I hope so. If you can get him to confess or resist arrest, we'll have something more substantial to charge him with. They say he' s got a temper. If he picks up something to throw, you know he's gone over the edge.

"Would you like to be there when Dom and Rich question him?" Bentley asked.

"Yes I would." Greg said. He looked forward to doing battle with a coward who picked on nice little old ladies. He grinned, as he thought of Gran's reaction to being called a little old lady.

"What's so funny?"

"Private joke. Want to come along? Greg asked.

"You betcha," Bentley replied as he stood and followed Greg to the door.
They radioed ahead and had Dom and Rich wait till they got there.

Dom and Rich, the uniformed officers, were waiting for them in the foyer of the Hexal office building.

"This guy must be important to rate two officers and two detectives. Do you want to question him?" Dom asked Greg.

"No, that's OK. Just make sure we do everything right. I don't want this arrest thrown out before we even get him to court," Greg said.

They rode the elevator to the eighteenth floor and when the doors opened on to the spacious reception area, made their way toward the desk and the beautiful young woman seated behind it.

"We'd like to speak with Sean Fitzsimmons." Dom said to the secretary.

She pressed the intercom switch. "Sir, there are some gentlemen here to see you."

"Send them in," Fitzsimmons said.

When he saw that the 'gentlemen' were two uniformed police officers and two detectives, he demanded, "What's going on? What's the idea of barging into my office?"

Dom stepped forward. "We'd like you to come down to the police station for questioning concerning the attempted murder of Penny MacIntyre."

Fitzsimmons' face went blank. "Who?"

"You probably know her as Gran," Dom said and started to read him his rights but when he finished there was no response.

"Do you understand?" Dom asked.

"What?"

"Do you understand?"

Fitzsimmons waved his hand as if trying to brush Dom away like a annoying fly. "Yes, yes, I understand." His head jerked up, "Wait a minute. Did you say attempted? You mean she's still alive?" he snarled. "How could she be? After all the trouble she's caused me, she'd better not be.

"That stupid woman is killing me. Every time she gets on television, every single time, our sales drop. Is that fair? She prances around and thinks she's so cool. I hate her! She has no right to criticize our products." He grabbed a heavy crystal vase full of flowers and threw it at the wall. It shattered and sent glass, water, and flowers down the wall and across the floor. He kicked at a large piece of glass and it flew through the air. Dom ducked just in time.

"Hey, knock it off, you jerk!" Dom yelled, as he reached for the CEO's arm.

Fitzsimmons kicked Dom and doubled him over. While everyone's attention was on Dom, Fitzsimmons grabbed a paperweight and flung it at Greg, who snatched it out of the air and was sorely tempted to throw it back at the CEO's head, but he refrained. Instead he spun Fitzsimmons around and handcuffed him.

The man became hysterical. "You can't do this to me!"

"Just watch me," Greg muttered.

"Don't you know who my father is?"

"When the newspapers get hold of this, it's not going to matter who your father is, *you're* going to be out of a job and, hopefully in jail."

Fitzsimmons, his face a mask of rage, threw himself at Greg, who stepped aside and allowed Fitzsimmons to collide with the wall. Rebounding from the wall, he lowered his head and charged Bentley. Bentley dodged and, looking at Greg. asked, "Can I shoot the idiot?"

"You guys are going to pay for this," Fitzsimmons shouted. "And I'm not through with that woman yet. She's not going to make a fool of me."

Just then, he looked up and noticed his staff was gathered in the reception area, staring at him. He glared at the two women who had volunteered to find someone to dispose of the old lady, "What are you looking at, you worthless bitches? Can't you do anything right? If you had done the job right, I wouldn't have had to get involved. She's still alive; did you know that?"

Greg motioned for Bentley to put the women under arrest; Rich helped Dom to his feet and they all marched down the hall and into the elevator.

Fitzsimmons tried to slam Greg against the elevator wall but Greg wrenched the CEO's arm higher and got a satisfying scream for his efforts.

Chapter 33

Gran couldn't pull into the newspaper office parking lot because a service truck was blocking the driveway. She was forced to park on the street half a block away by the empty baseball diamond.

The attempt on Gran's life had traumatized her to the point where Drew wouldn't let Gran out of her sight. They would quit following her when the bad guys were safely behind bars. It should be soon now, but until then, they were going to do their best to protect Gran. They parked at the top of the hill and watched as Gran got out of the jeep and walked across the street to the newspaper office. She turned in her column to the receptionist, said good-bye and closed the door behind her. She walked back across the grass. The tire tracks had been filled in, but the damage that had been done to the yard while trying to kill her could still be seen. *Why is all this happening? I'm just a cute little old lady who only wants people to be happy and healthy.* She crossed the street and started walking along the sidewalk towards her Jeep.

Bob's cell phone rang. "Hello," Bob said.

"We got them. He's being brought in as we speak," his brother Greg said. "But he did say something disturbing."

"What was that?"

"He said something about not being finished with her yet. Keep an eye on her just a little bit longer. Got to run." The sound of Greg hanging up sounded strangely ominous.

Chapter 34

Gran noticed there was a black SUV parked right behind her Jeep, so she circled in back of several trees so she could see if the car was empty or not. *I know I'm probably being paranoid. A person can't even park their car anymore without my being suspicious.* She came closer. There were two men in the car; both wore suits. She stood still trying to decide whether they were ordinary businessmen or if they posed a threat. One man turned his head toward her. *I'm going to look stupid running to hide behind the restrooms. But at least I'll be alive,* she thought, as she turned back and started to run toward the concrete building that housed the restrooms. The black SUV roared to life, backed up and jumped the curb, accelerating across the lawn.

The roar made Bob and Drew become instantly alert.

"Bob, there they are, look." She pointed at the black SUV. Bob quickly threw the shift into gear, drove down the hill, and tried to catch up with the SUV.

"What's that sticking out of the window? Is that a rifle?" Drew asked.

They heard a pinging sound. They looked over at Gran. She was still running. She had about 20 feet before she could dive behind the cement block building.

"It must be a dart gun. It would have to be if they want it to appear like a natural death," Bob said.

"They're shooting at her; Bob, stop them!" Drew yelled.

Bob drove up and over the curb; his wheels started spinning in the wet grass. Drew jumped out and started running. Her long legs ate up the distance.

She started to scream, "Stop, stop. Don't you dare hurt her."

The SUV slowed. There was another shot. Drew looked up. Gran was still moving. She reached the building and disappeared behind it.

"She's safe, thank God."

Bob gave up on the car and leaped out. He punched 'talk' on the cell phone as he ran after Drew. Before the man could turn and fire on Drew, she had reached him, wrenched the rifle away and used it to hit him. Blood flew from his face. She threw the rifle to the ground, grabbed the door handle, and yanked it open. She grabbed his collar and dragged him onto the ground. She kicked him, and then fell on him punching and pummeling him. Bob reached the back of the SUV. Police sirens filled the air.

"Drew, stop; you'll kill him."

Bob reached into the car and hauled out the other man before he could figure out what had happened and try to make his escape.

"Behave or I'll sic her on you."

The man looked down at his partner's bloody face and then at Drew, covered with his partner's blood, and fainted.

Drew did not wait until the police arrived. "I'll go tell Gran the coast is clear." She ran toward the cement block building.

"Gran, it's OK, you're safe."

As she rounded the corner she saw Gran lying face down on the grass.

"Gran, *Gran*, you can get up now." She knelt and shook Gran's shoulder. "Gran!" Alarm sounded in her head. She stood up and ran around the edge of the building. The fear was full blown now and she screamed. "Bob, my God, Bob, I think they killed her!"

A dart was sticking out of Gran's thigh. Drew turned back, knelt down beside her and pulled it out. Then she felt for her pulse; Gran's pulse was frantic under Drew's fingers; like the heart of a terrified bird.

"Bob help," she begged, just as Bob came around the corner. He knelt down and lifted Gran into his arms and ran to the SUV.

Greg was just arriving. He leaped from his car and started toward them.

"They shot her with a dart gun. Call the hospital and make sure they're ready for us," Bob yelled.

Greg pulled out his phone and dialed.

With a scream of sirens the ambulance arrived. Bob carried her over. Drew handed the dart to the med techs.

"I think it might be Thyroxin or thyroid; something like that, to overstress her heart, yet not able to be identified."

Drew leaped into the ambulance and off they went. The hospital was only two blocks away, so they barely got the oxygen on when they were wheeling her into the emergency room.

"Gran, please don't die, please don't die," Drew pleaded, as tears streamed down her face.

The orderly placed a stethoscope against Gran's chest.

"Wow, heart murmur big-time."

A small voice urged her to pray. *"Why would I do that? She thought, Wait, it worked for Karen. God, please make it work for Gran.*

When they reached the emergency doors, Bob was right behind them. Instead of staying with Gran, Drew flew into the hospital hallway and grabbing the first person she saw, yelled, "Where is the chapel?"

"The chapel? Sure, down the hall to the left." The orderly said.

"Thanks"

She ran down the hall, which smelled of disinfectant and blood. The blood smell was probably from her. She looked down. She was splattered. She ran to the water fountain, her bloody face reflected in the stainless steel. *No wonder I scared the guy.* She washed as best she could, while holding the faucet lever in with her stomach and the excess she wiped with the Kleenex she had in her pocket.

She opened the door of the chapel. It was empty and quiet. Light filtered though the high windows. She went and sat in the pew. She slid off the seat onto her knees. Tears flowed down her face and she made no effort to stop them.

"Please, God, please, Jesus, *please* heal my Gran. Please don't punish me for doubting you and for not being sorry I beat that slug of a man up. He was trying to kill my Gran. Father, I want to know you. I want to feel your power and I want to see your power surge through this place and heal her. I want you and Jesus in my life. Please tell me what to do." She visualized Jesus standing over Gran's hospital bed.

Please heal her. Just touch her. What's that we say in church before Communion?

"*Just say the word and I will be healed.*" *Please, Lord, say the word so that Gran will be healed.* Even though every instinct told her to run and be with Gran, she bowed her head and allowed her spirit to quiet.

A voice spoke to her, "Drew, I have called you by name. I love you. I will heal your grandmother. Have *faith* in me and in my word. Do not listen to the world's voices. I *will* heal her."

Papa stood beside Gran's bed. He clung to her hand. He had broken all speed limits to get there. His big booming voice had opened doors and intimidated nurses, so that he could now stand guard over his precious wife, his support, his shield, his little buddy. Bob stood behind Papa and Gran as a doctor sadly shook his head. "I'm sorry; we just couldn't counteract it in time." He reached up and closed Gran's eyes, "She's gone".

Tears filled Bob's eyes as he left the room and he went in search of Drew. He stopped several nurses and asked if they had seen her. Two nurses remembered a bloody young woman rushing toward the chapel. He continued sadly down the hall. He took a deep breath and reached for the handle of the chapel door. He didn't relish the idea of telling Drew about her grandmother. It was so hard to believe. Gran had always been so much alive. He opened the door just as Drew was walking up the aisle toward him. She was practically dancing. A broad smile was on her face.

"Drew, Honey, she's gone."

He waited for the collapse.

She shook her head. "No, you don't understand. God said he would heal her, your words are not true."

Bob did not know what to do or think. He followed her out of the chapel, "Honey, I know you loved her; I loved her too, but I watched her spirit leave her body. She's gone. Maybe God meant that she is in heaven with Him. You know, like that song, 'The Ultimate Healing'. Maybe that's what He meant"

"No, He said He would heal her and that I was not to listen to what the world says."

Bob didn't know what to say. He would love for God to heal Gran. He knew Jesus was capable of healing her. Look what he did for Lazarus; but he'd seen her die. They entered the ward. They hadn't had time to give Gran a room. Papa stood like a stone statue beside the gurney.

He still clung to Gran's hand although the warmth of Gran's body was rapidly fading.

"Penn, please don't leave me," he whispered.

She looked dead. Drew tried not to let that shake her newfound faith. She couldn't look at Papa or Bob or Gran. She closed her eyes and put her hands over Gran's heart.

"Oh Father God. I plead with you, come from the edges of the universe. Your child needs you. Lord Jesus, Lord of my life, send forth your Holy Spirit into this woman, your servant, and heal this heart and this body."

She wanted to whine like a child and say, *You promised*, so she did.

"Father, you promised, you promised, you promised. Gran, come back. Gran, *please* come back. I command you in the name of Jesus, come back."

She forced herself to visualize Jesus laying his hands on Gran's shoulders and healing her. She pushed away any thought that tried to undermine her picture of Jesus healing Gran.

The doctor, who had moved on to other patients, started back toward Drew, thinking she might be getting hysterical.

Papa had been praying as hard as Drew. He thought Gran's hands felt warmer but it must be his imagination. "Come on, Old Paint, please don't leave me." He lifted her hand to his lips and kissed it. It did feel warm; he thought he felt it move. By now orderlies, nurses, and other doctors were gathered around, each secretly hoping for a miracle.

"Come on, Lord, we need a miracle." One nurse said, then realized she had said it a loud.

Gran's lips moved. She smiled and opened her eyes. She didn't seem surprised to see the crowd around her bed. She looked up at Papa and mumbled, "Don't call me Old Paint."

Papa continued to hold her fingers to his lips and let his tears run unheeded down his face. "I promise."

Drew laughed. "Hallelujah," she yelled and jumped up and down. "Thank you, Jesus. Thank you. Thank you, Jesus; oh my God you *are* real, and Jesus is real and He has power, and He kept his promise, He healed my grandma. He *healed* my grandma."

Bob couldn't stop grinning. He had witnessed a miracle and his wife sounded like an evangelical preacher on TV. Bob felt like jumping up and down too, but fell to his knees instead. The others followed except the young doctor.

"I must have misdiagnosed."

Bob looked up at him. He reached out and pulled him to his knees.

"No, you didn't. You just witnessed the power of the living God reach down and touch your life forever. You'll never be the same again."

The young doctor shook his head in bewilderment, "You're right; she was dead, no pulse, no breath, no brain waves, clinically dead." He bowed his head. "Wow, God, that was awesome."

Gran smiled at Drew and reached out for her. Drew rose and leaned over to hug her grandmother. "Welcome back, Gran."

Gran's Yummy Super Healthy Chocolate Chip Cookies

1½ C organic brown sugar / raw sugar /
   or sucanat (dehydrated cane juice)
½ cup butter
½ cup Olive oil or organic canola
1 ½ teaspoon soda
1-teaspoon sea salt
1/8 cup sweetened cocoa powder (I recommend Ghirardelli)
2 teaspoons real vanilla (shake well before measuring)
2 eggs (free range)

Beat together till well-mixed
Add:
2 cups almond meal
½ cup ground flax seed (just under 1/3 of whole seeds will equal ½ cup ground)
¼ cup whole flax seed
1 cup whole grain flour (whole wheat or spelt)
2 cups rolled organic oats
Optional: two heaping tablespoons powdered bone meal
1 cup semi-sweet Chocolate chips
(Gran prefers milk chocolate chips even though semi-sweet are healthy and milk chocolate chips are not)
1 + cup of chopped walnuts, raw almonds or pecans

www.ingramcontent.com/pod-product-compliance
Lightning Source LLC
Chambersburg PA
CBHW072218170626
46813CB00003B/990